WHEN THE RAIN CAME

Also by Matt Eicheldinger

Matt Sprouts and the Curse of the Ten Broken Toes

Matt Sprouts and the Day Nora Ate the Sun

Matt Sprouts and the Search for the Chompy Wompers

Holes in My Underwear:
Over 100 Poems That Will Knock Your Socks Off

Sticky Notes:
Memorable Lessons from Ordinary Moments

WHEN THE RAIN CAME

New York Times bestselling author

MATT EICHELDINGER

The authorised representative in the EEA is Simon and Schuster
Netherlands BV, Herculesplein 96 3584 AA Utrecht,
Netherlands. (info@simonandschuster.nl)

Andrews McMeel Publishing
a division of Andrews McMeel Universal
1130 Walnut Street, Kansas City, Missouri 64106

www.andrewsmcmeel.com

26 27 28 29 30 GPS 10 9 8 7 6 5 4 3 2 1

Paperback ISBN: 979-8-8816-0513-1
Hardcover ISBN: 979-8-8816-0514-8

Library of Congress Control Number: 2025947668

Editor: Erinn Pascal
Art Directors: Tiffany Meairs and Julie Barnes
Production Editor: Kelsey Rolofson
Production Manager: Jeff Preuss
Cover Designer: Adrian Morgan
Special Thanks: Alessia Trunfio

ATTENTION: SCHOOLS AND BUSINESSES
Andrews McMeel books are available at quantity discounts
with bulk purchase for educational, business, or sales
promotional use. For information, please email the
Andrews McMeel Publishing Special Sales Department:
sales@andrewsmcmeel.com.

"Our most basic instinct is not for survival but for family."

—Paul Pearsall

Chapter 1

I used to rely on the weather to keep track of days. I could tell you Tuesday was an especially hot day because we were playing in the sprinklers, or Sunday was a little overcast so we stayed inside and watched a movie.

But now?

Now it is just constant, incessant, unrelenting rain.

It's hard to believe it's only been one month since it started. Every day bleeds together with the same atmosphere and mood as the day before. The only variety between drizzle and downpour is the occasional flash of lightning, but most days I can't tell the difference because I am more preoccupied with the rising water level. Last we heard, it's an average of an eighth of an inch a day, but that doesn't feel right considering the first floor of the mansion is now unusable, when just a few days ago I could escape there to be by myself.

Not anymore, though. Alone time is a thing of the past, and now I am in the continuous presence of Niko and Jada, my foster parents, or whatever I'm supposed to call them.

"Jada, hand me the scraper from the toolbox," Niko instructs as he holds out his hand. "I found more mold in the corner by the stairs."

Jada and I walk down the first few steps toward the first floor to hand Niko the scraper, which I think used to be a tool for painting. Now its only job is to chip away the black mold as it populates in the dark corners of the home. So, basically everywhere, since the sun hasn't been out in weeks.

"Remember when we first bought the mansion?" Jada asks Niko as she tiptoes onto a half-submerged step. "I told you it was too big to clean *then*, and it is certainly too big to clean *now*."

"True, but I also remember how enamored you were with all the storage space," Niko recalls as he drags the scraper against the corner of the wall. "And hasn't it come in handy?"

Niko is referring to the Bin Room. Well, Bin *Rooms*, actually. I didn't know what they were when I first arrived at the mansion, and I didn't ask because at that point, I'd never been with a family for more than just a few weeks before they backed out.

But then the rain came, and everything changed.

Jada pushes a string of damp hair behind her ear and glances in my direction. "You probably weren't even born yet when we bought this place. How old are you again, Aurora?"

"Seventeen," I say, while lifting my heels off the carpeted steps so I can hear the suction of the water under the base of my boots. "How old are you?"

"Old enough," Niko jokes as he motions toward the gray bucket I'm holding. "Why don't you throw that over the balcony before we all get sick from the smell?"

He is right. The smell of damp, moldy pieces of drywall in the bucket has a stench like you have your head in the opening of a sewer. I nod to Niko and pull my hood up as I walk back up the steps, down the hallway past the Bin Rooms, and toward the front of the mansion, where there's a sliding-glass door on the second-floor balcony.

There isn't too much to see today. The rain makes it difficult to glimpse more than a few yards ahead, and what's visible just looks like everything else these days.

Wet.

I push the sliding-glass door open and take a step outside. It does feel like an escape to be out here sometimes. The air inside the mansion is thick with moisture, which saturates the floors and walls with a thin layer of mist. So, really, the only thing that feels different outside is the sound.

"Please shut the door behind you!" Jada shouts from behind me. "It's damp enough in here already!"

But I can barely hear her.

Shouting is a new normal. You have to shout if you want to be heard over the rain and the rushing water between houses. When the rain first started, there was shouting, too, but for fun.

It was the start of summer when it first began, the type of rainy day you beg for when you've been outside in the heat all day. Jada and I had been in the front yard all afternoon stocking the bins with the new shipment of beans and rice, so when clouds formed and brought a downpour, it was easy to accept the cold relief from the heat. Kids came outside and played soccer, hooting and hollering at each other as puddles quickly formed on the sidewalk and low spots in the yards.

The next day the temperature dropped by almost thirty degrees, but neighbors and their kids continued to play in the street, which already had an inch of water. There were paper boats, obstacle courses for bikes, and some people even tried bringing out kayaks to navigate the water, which didn't work, but it was still enjoyable to laugh at their attempt.

Those are the only days I can remember during the rain that were fun. Everything since has added more chaos to this disaster, because it's not just raining here.

It's raining *everywhere.*

Chapter 2

That's the last of 'em," Niko announces as he shoves the last bin onto the shelf in Bin Room #5. "What's the current count?"

I flip to the second page on my clipboard and do the math in my head while my finger hovers over each box on Niko's spreadsheet.

Each bin has enough food for two people for two days. There are sixteen bins left, which should cover thirty-two days. But since I was not part of the equation when Niko and Jada started prepping years ago, sixteen bins only feed *three* people for . . .

"Twenty days, if we don't ration it," I say, tapping the clipboard and showing the math to Niko. "Twenty-five if we do."

"It could be worse," he admits, looking out the window. "I'm sure most families ran out of food weeks ago."

We could have helped them. We *should* have helped them. There are enough supplies here to keep many families going, but that would be breaking their number one rule of prepping: *You prep for you, and no one else. No one.*

I didn't know Niko and Jada were preppers until a full week after I arrived at their home. Some might call them survivalists, but that term seems too dignified for what they are. Survivalists are live-off-the-land, figure-it-out sort of people, but Niko and Jada?

They just bought stuff.

And they bought a *lot* of it.

"With Niko's background as an engineer and mine as an architect, we understand the importance of planning. Everything should have a purpose. You have to be prepared for anything, any disaster situation," Jada lectured as she toured me around the mansion during my first week living here, back before the rain came. "Two is one, one is none."

"What does that mean?" I asked, staring at the stacked bins that lined the wall of an open room.

"It's rule number two of prepping," she said as she closed the door and led me to another one. "You need to have a backup plan. If something breaks or fails and you only had one, you now have none."

"Oh, okay," I said. "What is rule number one, then?"

"You prep for you, and no one else," she said firmly. "*No one.*"

When it became clear the rain wasn't going to stop anytime soon, it was like a switch flipped inside Niko's and Jada's heads. Their demeanor changed completely, and everything became a task or mission.

"I've been on the ham radio all morning," Niko said during breakfast on the tenth day of heavy rain. That was how he communicated with other preppers—on the ham radio, a two-way communication device. "We all agree this is a Bug-In scenario."

"That means we are staying here for now," Jada whispered to me as Niko dropped his fork and began to sketch in his notebook. "Bug-Out means we leave."

"Oh," I replied. "Um, can I listen to the radio with you sometime?"

"No, and don't touch it either."

The answer came out of Niko about as fast as I thought it would.

"Do we have a place to Bug-Out to?" I continued. "Does anyone?"

Niko stopped sketching furiously and looked up at me.

"Rule number five of prepping," he muttered, slowly tapping the tip of his pencil on the table. "If we have a Bug-Out location, we don't speak of it until we need it."

Niko looked a lot younger before it started raining. Back then, his light-brown hair flipped above his head like a model's. Now, it was weighed down by the mist and humidity, and it was usually plastered to his forehead, which was starting to make it difficult to interpret his expressions.

"Let's talk about something else," Jada said. "Now, Aurora, I've tried multiple times to contact the foster care center, but I can't seem to get through to anyone."

"Are you sending me back there?" I brusquely asked.

"Of course not!" Jada quickly responded as she tried to catch Niko's attention. "We just want to . . . make sure they know you are safe."

"I doubt the grid is functional anyway. If we don't have electricity here, I doubt anyone does," Niko grumbled. "Good thing we have the genny."

"The what?" I asked.

"The generator," Jada said. "It's powered by gas and creates electricity."

"And the 'grid'?" I continued.

"The system that delivers electricity to the city. I used to work on projects like that," Niko said, putting his pencil down. "I think that is enough questions for one morning. Let's begin training for the day."

Of all the strange things Niko and Jada started when the rain came, training was perhaps the strangest. It revolved around three categories: BOB, IFAK, and EDC.

BOB stands for "Bug-Out-Backpack." It's a backpack filled with essential survival items you can quickly grab if you have to leave in a hurry. We each have multiple stored across the mansion in different rooms so we can easily find one in case of an emergency. All of my BOBs are different shades of green and contain the same things: food, water, matches, batteries, and a flashlight. Every few days the three of us empty each backpack to make sure everything is in working order, which includes the IFAK.

IFAK stands for Individual First Aid Kit. Jada has been teaching me how to care for different wounds and diseases, which freaks me out more than the rain. The thought of having to stitch my own wound is nauseating, and I get sick to my stomach every time we go through another tutorial. I don't think Niko likes it either, which is why he is in charge of my EDC training.

EDC stands for Everyday Carry, which are the items I should have on me at all times. Most of my early EDC training was spent checking to make sure I was carrying everything I was supposed to, but one day, Niko added something new.

"Do you have everything before we start?" Niko asked. "Count them out."

"One, multitool. Two, lighter. Three, flashlight," I confirmed.

"And today we are adding a fourth."

Niko reached behind his back, underneath his shirt, and pulled out something I hadn't seen before.

"An axe?" I asked, stunned. "Why would I need that?"

"Technically, it's a hatchet," he said matter-of-factly. "Let's head to the loft."

I followed Niko up the next flight of stairs to a small loft that overlooked part of the second floor.

This was where I'd soon do the majority of my EDC training, like how to start a fire or make a simple trap with a knife. It also served as my new bedroom, since the last one was now completely underwater on the first floor.

"If this rain doesn't stop soon," Niko said as he revealed a second hatchet strapped to his chest underneath his shirt, "people will go looking for supplies. Looters, thieves. They'll all want what we have."

"Then what is the axe—I mean, the hatchet—for?" I asked again.

"Protection," Niko said, and then in one swift motion turned and threw his hatchet, sinking it into a wooden vertical support beam at the center of the loft.

"You expect me to do *that*?"

"If people come inside our home, then yes," Niko declared as he removed his hatchet from the beam.

"But what if . . ." I hesitated. "What if they have a gun?"

"Won't matter," Niko said as he slowly ran his thumb over the blade of the hatchet. "With all this moisture in the air, most guns aren't going to fire. You can't keep them dry enough, so they rust."

"How do you know that?" I asked.

"Because all of *mine* are rusted," Niko said almost apologetically as he walked back toward the front of the loft. "So, I can't teach you how to shoot even if I wanted to. Instead, we have the hatchet."

"But I can hardly throw a football," I said. "How am I ever going to hit anything with a hatchet?"

Niko took a few steps back and threw his hatchet at the beam again, hitting it in almost the exact same spot as before.

"You're going to practice. A lot," he said.

I couldn't help but wonder what Niko and Jada would be like if we weren't trapped in this disaster. I don't expect anyone to be perfect, but showing any sort of feeling that they want me around would be nice.

"Maybe we could play a game instead?" I suggested. "Do you have any board games or cards? I know how to play rummy."

Niko didn't even bother to look in my direction while I was talking. Instead, he walked up to the beam and yanked the hatchet out again.

"Here," he said, flipping the hatchet in his hand so the handle was facing me. "Now let's get started."

Chapter 3

The nightly noises are beginning to change now.

For the past month since the rain came, the sounds have been fairly predictable. It is the sound of the rain, obviously, but also a bit more. After hearing it daily for weeks, my ears have now adjusted, and I've started to make out things I couldn't before, like floating empty cans clattering against each other on the rivers between buildings, window glass breaking as the water rises and pushes into new territory, and now—the screams.

The haunting screams.

They aren't close to the mansion, but they don't seem far away either. The shrieks are just enough of a jolt to keep you from falling into a deep sleep, and my hand automatically darts toward my hatchet each time I hear a scream, even though I don't plan on throwing it at anyone.

Even so, I decide it's probably best to tell Jada about the changing noises during breakfast. But her attempt to soothe me doesn't really help.

"It's just the animals fighting for higher ground." Jada says from the safety of our kitchen.

I say *kitchen,* but it's really just a few gray folding tables we moved to the other side of the living room. The actual kitchen went underwater two weeks ago, so this temporary one is all we have.

"I'm sure it's just a raccoon, or maybe a cat," Jada continues.

"You and I both know it's not animals," Niko says bluntly, looking firmly at Jada. "This is why we are keeping the lights off as much as possible now, especially at night. I want this place to appear like it has nothing to offer to anyone. I want us to be invisible."

The silence that follows hangs in the air until I get the nerve to ask a question.

"So, is this a Bug-Out situation, then?" I ask. "Should we leave?"

Their spoons keep scraping on the bowls as the two of them continue to eat, as if they haven't heard a thing I've said.

I don't ask again.

Instead, I finish my cereal and water (because we ran out of milk weeks ago), and I ascend the small staircase to the loft and pull out my hatchet.

With nothing else to do than chores, watching the blade sink into the grains of that same wooden beam is satisfying enough to keep me coming back on my own. And after a month of practicing, I am getting better.

Left foot forward.

Tight grip, with the thumb resting upward on the handle.

One swift motion . . .

THWAK!

"That sounded like a powerful throw!" Niko shouts from below. "You must be improving!"

I go up to the beam to see how far the blade has penetrated the wood.

Two inches. Not bad.

"It's in there pretty good!" I shout back, and peer over the railing for their approval. "Going for accuracy today, though!"

"It's always good to have a goal, Aurora!" Jada declares in a seemingly rare moment of motherly advice. "Don't you think, Niko?"

But Niko is now messing with the buttons of the ham radio, oblivious to the conversation that Jada is trying to include him in.

"I said, *don't you think, Niko?*" Jada repeats.

"Yeah, sure," he says. "Always."

I continue throwing the hatchet, even hours after Niko and Jada leave the kitchen to complete their chores. Once their voices are gone, the only things I can hear are the rain and the rhythmic sound of the hatchet hitting the wood.

THWAK!

THWAK!

THWAK!

Until something new interrupts it.

A buzzing sound, coming up from the kitchen.

I look over the railing and see the ham radio on the table. I never see it without Niko within earshot, so I wait for him to show up.

Minutes go by.

He doesn't.

I pull my hatchet out of the beam and creep down the steps until I am close enough to hear the radio more clearly. You can barely make out the exact sound between the different tones of static, but it is unmistakable.

It is a voice!

A human voice!

Up until this moment, I haven't heard another person, aside from Niko and Jada, in weeks. The laughter of neighborhood kids is gone. The older man who walked his dog each morning is gone. The only human activity I've seen is an orange emergency flare someone shot into the sky one evening, when I happened to be on the balcony dumping moldy drywall.

Even in that emergency, there hadn't been a voice to go with it. But there is one now. It's cutting in and out, and even through the static, I know what a panicked voice sounds like.

"Are you . . . emergency broadca—through the . . ."

What are they saying?!

I've seen Niko work the ham radio enough to know how to turn up the volume, but I have no idea how to work the other components. I twist the largest knob clockwise first, which makes the radio crackle.

"*Prep—*"

I immediately turn it the other way, which gives the same result.

"*Par—*"

Instead of continuing to fiddle with the first dial, I take the second knob, the smaller of the two, and twist it counterclockwise just in time to hear the voice on the other end say, this time perfectly clear:

"*Preparations for your departure to The Hill are underway. Stand by for further instructions.*"

"WHAT ARE YOU DOING WITH MY RADIO?!"

Niko suddenly appears from the east hallway. His tone is something I've never heard out of him before. Stern, low, and powerful. I freeze, my hand still on the second knob.

"*My radio,*" Niko repeats firmly, pushing his wet hair to the side. "Did you hear anyone?"

It's easy to lie when you know you are about to be in trouble, so that's what I do. I lie.

"I thought I heard a voice, so I came down to get a better listen, but it was just static."

"You sure about that?" Niko insists, grabbing the radio. "It's important I know what is going on. If you heard or said anything, I would need to—"

A sudden bang comes from outside the house.

A second one follows.

Then a third.

The rhythmic banging continues as Niko and I stare toward the nearest window, a view of what was once the garden, from the second floor. Jada appears from the hallway, looking at us as if we have an answer for the noise.

"What is it?" I ask, one hand on my hatchet.

Niko holds his finger to his lips and moves toward the window, his hand gripping the hatchet on his own hip. Even though it's still morning, you would never know because the clouds and rain block most of the light from reaching the water. Everything outside that was once bright and colorful is now dulled, almost like an old black-and-white film.

Niko looks down, and his posture changes. He removes his hand from the hatchet.

"It's okay," he announces. "But I'd advise you not to look."

Jada heeds his warning and stays perfectly still. However, I take a few steps forward to join Niko at the window and look below.

He doesn't have to point out what was making the noise. When I look down, it is obvious.

There, floating in the water, bobbing up and down with the current as it slams against the top of the door below us, is the body of a dead deer.

Its antlers are barely visible, but the small white patch underneath its tail makes it easy to spot. Its fur is completely matted, like someone has soaked the deer in oil, and its body seems to be bloated, as the stretch marks of the pink underside of its belly show. Each small wave of water pulls the deer back before sending it forward again, pounding into the doorframe like a slow, powerful knock.

Then, Niko moves his finger toward the corner of the window to show something else.

I look beyond the deer. There, collecting in the middle of the street among the swirling water, are more deer corpses. Dozens of them.

Floating.

And while we're not dead like them, it's hard to say we're *living*, either.

We are just here.

Drifting in place.

Floating.

Just floating.

Chapter 4

"Aurora, will you please roll this barrel down the east hallway to the last door?" Jada asks later that day, tapping the side of the barrel like a drum. "I want to get the rest of these moved before evening."

Niko motions for me to do the same. There won't be talk of what we saw outside earlier; there never is. I learned this quite quickly once the water rose and Niko and Jada started acting differently. It was like everything we saw or heard that should create a large conversation didn't, and instead, the two of them treated the scenario as if it was expected.

After the first week of rain, when we gathered together to watch the news and learned it was happening across the entire globe, Niko and Jada just sat there.

The second week, when scientists declared that the rain was an "unprecedented global disaster," we didn't talk about it. We organized the food.

And the third week, when it was clear from the news that the government couldn't help anyone and people were looting the stores, neither of them spoke. They did, however, lock the doors.

And just last week, when the distant sound of explosions started, they didn't talk about that either. They just continued to prep and check all our supplies.

I say *our* supplies, but it doesn't feel that way all the time. More and more, I feel like I am an extra piece, one that doesn't quite fit. I think they care for me, or else they wouldn't have taken me in.

But I just wish I could *feel* it.

"Quickly now, Aurora," Jada prompts, pointing to the barrel again as I sit there, haunted by the visual of the dead deer. "Niko and I have more to do."

I know we don't talk about things as they happen. But I need to talk. I need to talk about what we just saw.

"Actually, do you think . . ." I hesitate. "Do you think maybe we could just sit together for a while? I don't feel very good after seeing . . . that."

I don't need to specify what "that" is.

Jada pauses. Her hands still for just a second on the lid of a barrel. She glances at Niko, who is tightening a rope along the ceiling beams, then looks back at me.

"There's still so much to do," she says, but this time, her voice is softer, almost regretful.

Niko exhales sharply. "We'd like to, Aurora. Really. But if we don't keep up with this . . ." He gestures to the stacked supplies, the moldy walls, and the water seeping in along the seams of the floor. "We can't afford to fall behind."

Jada steps closer to me, like she wants to do something else. A hug would be nice. When was the last time I had a hug?

Instead, she just presses her lips together, then turns back to the barrels.

I nod like I'm not disappointed, like I wasn't hoping for something else.

Caring isn't the same as fully embracing someone else, making them feel like they belong. But in moments like this, I wonder if any of us really have a choice in whether we belong. Especially me.

I grab the tall, empty blue barrel and roll it down the hallway. Even though I've lived here for over a month, I still get confused in the hallways because of all the doors. Some I know—like the Bin Rooms, where the food is kept. Or the BOB Room, where there are extra supplies like flashlights, water bottles, and backpacks.

But there are other doors that I've never seen open because they are locked, like the one I have to roll the barrel to. It's labeled INCH ROOM.

Jada and Niko are now in the living room. It's not too far, so I can still see them. Jada is fumbling with a small black crate, and Niko has his ear pressed up to the ham radio.

"Just place it against the wall and come get another!" Jada yells as she struggles to move the crate.

"Coming!" I shout back, and stand the barrel against the south wall. The air shoots up between the wall and side of the barrel—a foul, musty odor, like when you walk into the locker room of a public pool that hasn't been cleaned in days. It's a smell that makes the inside of my nose feel as moldy as everything else.

I fan the air away with one hand. Then I look back at the door of the INCH Room. Curiosity gets the better of me, and I let my other hand graze the doorknob. I turn it to see if it is still locked. It is.

I have no idea what INCH means, and I don't plan on asking either. If they won't unlock the door, I don't expect they will tell me anything about it.

All the other doors in the mansion remind me of the previous families I've stayed with. One door has a scratch on the bottom, which was like the second home with all the dogs. Another door looks older than the others, like the fourth house I stayed in, where *everything* was old.

I've been in eight different foster homes over the years, that I can remember, anyway. When you get bounced around to so many places—and get stuck back at the agency in between them—all the details blur together into one giant fog of half memories, and it can be hard to remember when you were where.

But I do know one thing for certain. None of the families I've stayed with have ever come close to becoming permanent.

That is, until Niko and Jada. Or so I thought.

It was their letter that made me think they were different.

I remember the way the envelope felt in my hands, the paper slightly crumpled from being passed between too many people before finally reaching me. My name was scripted neatly across the front in dark ink.

Aurora

No last name. No case number.

Just me.

I hesitated before opening it, half expecting some official notice, another set of instructions, another temporary placement. But inside, the words weren't cold or impersonal. They weren't clipped sentences typed onto a form.

They were real. Thoughtful. Handwritten.

Hello, Aurora.

We hope this letter finds you well. We wanted to write and let you know that we've been thinking about you. We enjoyed meeting you the other day, and if you'd like, we would be honored to welcome you into our home, our family.

Family.

The word made something in my chest tighten, like a muscle I hadn't stretched in too long. Had anyone ever used that word—*family*—with me before? I didn't think so. That I would have remembered. *Our family* wasn't a promise, not exactly, but it wasn't nothing either.

I read the letter over and over, tracing the curves of their words with my fingers as if touching them could make them real. No one had ever written to me before.

I wanted to believe in the hope laced between those sentences.

I wanted to believe they meant it.

And when I arrived at their home, I could *feel* it. I could actually feel it.

The warmth of Jada's greeting. The kindness in Niko's smile. It was real.

But then the rain came and washed all of that away in an instant.

The promise of becoming a family was replaced by the fear of falling apart and being put right back where I've always been. Alone.

"I need to find a better place to listen," Niko declares a few moments later while I'm still hauling barrels. He and Jada have left the living room and are standing in the hallway again, Niko's ear still pressed up against the ham radio. "Lots of chatter coming through today."

"What is the latest report of the city?" Jada asks.

Niko holds the radio to his face and adjusts one of the dials, then places it on top of one of the standing barrels. "The city was lost weeks ago. You know that. It's a disaster zone."

Jada curls her face up, as if she hadn't heard. "And news from the state?"

"There is no state," Niko says, almost cutting her off. His voice is sharp, and his glare is sharper. "No one has a state. No one has a city. No one has a town. That time of life is over. It's over!" He exhales, shaking his head. "You think there's order left somewhere? That someone's keeping the lights on in Des Moines or Minneapolis? That some governor's got a plan? There's nothing. Just water and whatever's left floating in it. And the plans we have made to stay safe." He leans forward now, lowering his voice but not quite softening it. "Even the ones who climbed high enough to stay dry in the other states, like Colorado, like Montana. They're *still drowning.* Drowning in fear, in hunger, in the kind of madness that comes when the world stops making sense. It is only people like us, people who planned, who have a chance."

Jada looks over at me and then back at Niko.

"So, when do you think we are going to—" Jada halts abruptly before finishing her question. Niko stops rotating the dials like he is about to respond, then tightens his mouth, grabs the radio, and walks down the hallway.

It's an odd interaction. But most of our conversations are like that now, anyway.

"You know what?" Jada says to me. "Why don't I get the rest of these barrels and you can take a break. Maybe find a book to read in the library?"

"Um, okay," I say, stunned that I don't have to do more chores. "Where is that again?"

"Same hallway as Niko. Second door on the right," she instructs, and then rolls another barrel away.

Reading. It is strange to be told to do something for entertainment, to *read,* when every day for the last month has been about survival. I almost forgot about it. Reading.

I have only been in the library once before, when Jada gave me the first tour. Even then, I only got to peek over her shoulder into the room as she told me which famous authors she'd met over the years. She was really active in book clubs, from what I've heard. Always volunteering at the local library for events, and even coordinating author visits for local schools. The last event she did before the rain came was with Lois Lowry, who happens to be the author of my favorite book, *The Giver.* But I didn't tell Jada that at the time. It was too early to open up, too early to try and get close.

Now, I wish I had. I might never get the chance to do it again.

In any case, if I have to guess, there are probably no books for anyone my age in Niko and Jada's library, but at least it will be something different to do.

I make my way to the library and open the door, my hatchet bouncing in the sheath against my hip with each step. At first glance, the library seems like a small room, but it has the most books I've ever seen in one place outside of a public school or city library. Two long bookshelves line the walls on both sides of the room.

Maybe I can actually find something in here to read.

I scan the first bookshelf.

The Art of War by Sun Tzu.

A Confederacy of Dunces by John Kennedy Toole.

Two books I've never heard of before. Not a great start. So I go to the other shelf.

Lord of the Flies by William Golding.

The cover is immediately enticing because of its red streaks and obscured face, but what pulls me in more is the small text on the bottom: "Afterword by Lois Lowry."

Well, if my favorite author read it, I guess I'll give it a shot.

I turn toward the biggest window I've seen in the house so far, which is wedged between the two bookshelves in the middle of the room. It is a bay window, with a large built-in lounge, and I can almost feel the pull of it to sit down and look outside. Since all the other windows in the house are flat against the wall, it is hard to see far in any direction other than straight out or down. This window, however, sticks out past the siding of the mansion, which means I might be able to see farther, or maybe at least something new.

And hopefully not the dead deer again.

I curl up in the corner of the lounge chair and press my face against the pane of glass. It's always colder by the windows, so I pull my hands into my sweatshirt for warmth. Even though it is almost noon, there is barely enough light coming through the clouds to see the neighborhood, or what is left of it. The dark water doesn't allow you to see anything beneath it, just what is above or about to go under.

I can just make out the two houses across the street, and they are in poor shape. Both are smaller than Jada and Niko's mansion, and the water seems to run *through* these houses rather than *around* them.

I can't see the front door of the first house because the awning above it has collapsed, which must be why there is a large visible hole in the center of the home. All the windows on its first floor are shattered as well, and since the gutters have ripped off the roof, a giant waterfall is cascading off it and splashing into the moving water below. That's likely some of the sloshing I've been hearing, at least.

The house next to it is in better shape, but only barely. Some peeling paint, a slightly collapsed roof near the chimney. And no signs of anyone.

I feel my hands get clammy.

Is that next for this place? How can we survive like that?

I look to the right, where the kids played in the street only a few weeks ago, back when the rain was simply creating puddles. Now, it's a swath of mixed debris, slowly swirling with no clear direction. There are large sticks, chairs, and trash cans that seem to be held together by some invisible force.

Suddenly, a streak of lightning jets across the sky, followed by a large, all-consuming bright flash. It's brief, but bright enough to light up the entire neighborhood.

That's when I see it.

Just before the light dissipates.

Across the street, between the decrepit house and the one next to it.

A boat.

A single aluminum boat.

And hanging off the side of it is . . .

Someone.

Chapter 5

At first, I thought other people were hunkering down in their homes, like us. Sometimes I'd catch another face pressed against the window across the street, and other times, when the water was lower, I could see someone walking through the street with all their belongings above their head or in waterlogged backpacks.

Niko called those people the "walking dead," since there isn't a change in elevation for miles and miles and they have nowhere to go. I thought they'd go to the city, but Niko quickly rejected that idea.

"If you want to put yourself in the worst situation possible, then sure, head to the city. But you'll see a darker side of people than you would think."

"Don't scare her like that," Jada protested. "We don't need to think of these things."

"We *do* need to think of these things," Niko hammered on. "The city will be taken over by those who have taken over *others*. The city is a death trap. A concrete, flooded death trap."

But we are not in the city. We are in a neighborhood, miles away from the danger Niko spoke of that day.

And whoever this man outside is, clinging to the boat, he is not a threat or danger to any of us. He is a human, and he is in trouble.

The lightning flashes again and illuminates the sky, and I can catch the outline of the man struggling to get into the boat.

The water seems deeper now, thicker. The wind is picking up, too, battering the boat against the frame of the house, pinning the man against the wall and the hull of the boat.

He needs help! He isn't going to make it!

"Jada!" I yell, turning my face toward the library door. "Get in here quick!"

The sound of fast-paced footsteps gets closer and closer until Jada finally arrives and joins me at the bay window.

"There!" I say, pointing in the direction of the boat. "Do you see him?"

Jada moves her head side to side like she can see around the pouring rain. Then she pushes her finger against the window.

"Right there?" she asks. "Is that a . . . person?"

"I think so!" I reply. "I think he is trying to get into that boat."

"That's . . . hard to watch," Jada admits as she stands back up. "We should probably go find something else to do. Did you pick out a book to read?"

“Wait, we aren’t going to help?!” I ask, shocked, as I drop my book onto the floor. “What if he is hurt?”

Jada looks down at the book, then to me, and then back toward the window. Her shoulders drop, which makes me realize how tight my own shoulders are.

“I want to, Aurora, I do,” she says as she brings one hand to her cheek to comfort herself. “But we can’t . . . we just can’t.”

“We *can* help!” I plead. “We have supplies! We have food! Why can’t we save him?!”

Jada slowly folds her arms around herself, gripping tightly around her waist as if she’s in quiet agony.

“Well, maybe we could get a rope,” she begins. “But then we would have to—”

“No,” a voice announces. “Rule number one.”

Niko is standing in the doorway, unshaken.

He saunters toward the window and looks out at the man, who now only has one hand on the frame of the boat as the waves continue to thrash him against the brick wall of the house.

We all watch for a moment, but not a word is spoken.

Niko then grabs the tops of the curtains on either side of the window and pulls them together, as if that will stop what’s happening outside.

“*No!*” I shout. I grab the bottoms of the fabric and try to rip them back open. “We can’t just sit here and watch! We need to help him!”

“Aurora, don’t!” Niko shouts back.

The curtains move an inch or two, but Niko holds his ends tighter and pulls them again, this time with much more force.

The yank sends me to the ground, the sleeve of my sweatshirt somehow ripping in the process.

"Niko! You cut her!" Jada yells as she looks over my forearm underneath the ripped sleeve. "What are you doing?!"

Jada helps me off the floor, and I furiously glare at Niko. He's frozen, his eyes locked on my arm.

"It's not a cut," I explain as I get to my feet. "It's just a birthmark. I'm okay."

Jada runs her hands over the three distinct brown dots arranged in a straight line on my forearm. They are equally spaced, like they were put there on purpose, but of course they were not. I've had them as long as I can remember, and I even have a name for them: "Orion's Belt," just like the constellation.

"Aurora, I'm . . . I'm so sorry," Niko stutters, backing up as his gaze darts away from me. His posture has changed, as if he has been defeated, or maybe just relieved that I'm not actually hurt. "I didn't mean for that to happen. Truly."

Before I can say another word, though, Niko straightens himself and puts his hand in front of his face, holding up just one finger.

"It's just . . . rule number one," he repeats. "We help *no one*."

With that, he turns and disappears down the

hallway, leaving Jada and me standing together. Not another word is spoken as the rain pelts against the window, the water continues to rise, and the curtains remain closed.

Chapter 6

I do not stay in the library after Niko leaves. I pull my sweatshirt hood over my damp hair and return to my loft.

As soon as I'm upstairs, I snatch the hatchet off my hip and launch it toward the center beam. It soars right past the beam and into the back of the loft, piercing into the side of a cardboard box that sits on top of a small coffee table.

THWACK!

I don't even care that I missed.

Instead of retrieving the hatchet, I flop on the mattress and stare up at the ceiling. Even though I only have a single bulb in an uncovered lamp to light the loft, I can see the sparkle of small water droplets forming on the rafters. *A leak.* This leak is new, and I should probably tell Niko or Jada, but right now, I don't care. I don't care about myself, and I don't care about them.

The only thing I care about is the man in the water.

It's not fair.

It's not right.

But like most things in my life, I don't get a choice. That's how it has always been. Go to one foster home. Leave. Go to another one. Leave that one too. And most likely, I am just here until I am moved somewhere else, if the rain ever stops.

Assuming there's even a dry place left to send me.

I lie in bed for the rest of the afternoon and into the evening, and neither Jada nor Niko makes any requests for me to do anything. I accidentally left the one book that seemed interesting back in the library, but I'm not going back for it. I don't want to see Niko on my way. It's not worth it.

Instead, I spend time looking at some old prepper magazines Jada gave me after the first floor flooded. They are mostly catalogs trying to sell things, like one of twenty different hunting knives or the best portable water purification system. I am not sure why Jada decided to keep them, because, as she told me before, "We bought all of it, just in case."

Later in the evening, I can hear Jada and Niko making dinner in the makeshift kitchen below, but I am not hungry. It doesn't feel right to eat when I know someone else is suffering. Plus, I am tired of the same repetitive food of canned beans, mushy vegetables, and rice—the prepper staples.

"Aurora?" Jada's voice calls out above the sound of the rain, breaking the silence and slightly echoing in the loft. "Can I come visit?"

Jada has never asked to enter the loft before. That's something.

"Sure," I reply, sitting up as a single drop of water falls from the rafter and hits my elbow.

Jada's head appears first, and before she climbs the stairs any farther, she takes a long look at me.

I take a long look at her too. I'm not sure how old she actually is. Her face doesn't have many wrinkles, but her hair is peppered with grays, which looks cool. I like that she doesn't dye it. You wouldn't know how wealthy she is by looking at her either. She doesn't wear excessive jewelry or makeup. Never has, it seems. (There were photos in the house before the flooding.) She climbs higher now, and I can see that her cargo pants seem to weigh her down, although the shell of her rain jacket makes it hard to see her actual build. But I'm quite sure she's very fit. There was a spin bike and full weight set in the garage, before the rain came, that she used "every day."

"I thought you might like some dinner," she says softly.

She slowly comes up the rest of the steps and takes a seat at the end of my mattress, handing me a plate filled with baked beans, rice, and something new: chicken.

"Where did you get this?" I ask, shoving one of the chicken strips into my mouth quickly, before she can answer. The immediate warmth of oil and grease sends my body into a frenzy, and I push a second piece in while still finishing the first, attempting to talk as I do. "I thought we only had beans and rice."

"We have a small supply of some vacuum-sealed meats," Jada says. "We just didn't want to eat it first."

"Well, it's really good," I add as I put the last piece in my mouth. I feel a bit guilty sitting here, eating a warm meal when that man might still be out there.

Jada smiles softly and lifts her own plate, which I didn't even notice she had, and tilts it toward mine, pushing her portion of chicken onto it.

"No, you don't have to do that," I say, and attempt to push it back. "You need to eat too."

"That's okay. I want you to have it," she affirms as she mixes her beans and rice together. "It's been a long, draining day, and you need your strength too."

Her voice is light and gentle, almost soothing. Like how I'd imagined it in her letter.

She raises her hand and holds it above my shoulder for a moment, like it's stuck in midair and doesn't know what to do. Then she places it gently on my shoulder and rubs it back and forth.

And for the first time since the rain began, I cry.

The simple presence of her touch is enough to break my dam, letting all the emotions of the past month pour out.

"I know," Jada assures me. "I feel the same way."

"I'm sorry," I say, wiping my eyes with my ripped sweatshirt sleeve. "I'm not sure why I'm crying."

"This isn't something people are prepared to deal

with, especially not kids," she points out. "But I suppose you've grown a lot this past month. I've seen it."

I push another run of tears off my face and look up at Jada, who is grinning.

"Oh, Aurora," she continues. "You've learned so much in such a short amount of time. You should be very proud of yourself. I certainly am."

I smile. I've learned to survive without compliments, but sometimes, I need them. I take another bite of chicken as Jada continues to rub her hand across the upper part of my back. No one has ever been this kind to me before. No one.

She takes a slow breath, then looks at me—not just at me, but into me, like she's searching for the right words.

"Aurora," she starts, her voice softer than I've ever heard it, "Niko and I . . . we've wanted this for a long time. To bring someone in. To have a family that wasn't just the two of us."

My chest tightens.

"But we never felt ready," she continues. "Never thought we'd know how to do it the right way. And as we got older, we realized that waiting wasn't an option anymore." She exhales, removes her hand from my back, and rubs her palms together. "I won't lie to you. We aren't perfect at this. We've never been parents before, and we're figuring it out as we go."

I stare at a loose thread on the mattress, running it between my fingers.

"It's okay," I say.

Jada shifts closer, her shoulder brushing mine.

"No, it's *not* okay." Her voice tightens with fervor. "Because you matter to us, Aurora. You really do. You deserve the absolute best, even in this unfortunate scenario."

I swallow hard as my emotions build.

"We're doing everything we know of to keep you safe. *Everything.* We are trying to figure out a plan. All I need from you is to give us some time and to let us earn your trust." She places her hand over mine, her grip firm, steady. "Can you do that?"

Her words settle deep in my chest, tangled up with every doubt and fear I've carried for as long as I can remember.

I *want* to believe her. I want to trust her. But trust has never come easy.

Jada suddenly looks up and shields her head with her other hand, spotting the fresh leak.

"Looks like we have a new problem, don't we?" she asks, pointing toward the rafters above. "Did you know about this?"

"I saw the drips earlier," I admit. "Sorry I didn't say anything."

"No, no, that's okay," she says. "Guess I better go tell Niko. Looks like we will have some more chores to do tomorrow, won't we?"

I sniff back the tears that make their way down my face but continue to smile through it.

I hadn't realized how much I really needed to hear all of this.

Jada rubs my shoulder one last time, grabs our empty dishes, and begins to descend the stairs to the kitchen, but not before taking one more look in my direction.

"Good night," I manage to say. "I'll see you in the morning. And thank you."

The "thank you" seems to break her. Jada rushes back into the loft, embracing me in a hug that feels like a necessity. A *hug*. An actual hug.

More tears spill out, and not just from me.

From Jada too.

It is a much-needed feeling, this moment of calm and understanding, and it lingers even after she's gone.

I stand up to peer over the edge of the loft and into the kitchen. Jada walks over to Niko and rubs his back as he dunks the dirty dishes from dinner into a bucket of soapy water. He pauses for a moment, and I watch his muscles relax as Jada rests her head on his shoulder, and the two of them stand quietly still together.

It's sweet. And it's the first time I've seen them show any affection toward each other. I wonder if there was a lot more of this before the rain came.

I head back over to my mattress, place my EDC items on the ground, and change out of my moist clothes and into the shorts and T-shirt I keep in the plastic bag near my pillow so they don't get wet from the damp air.

The leak is still going, so I jam an old towel into the hole. That should work for now, and hopefully through the rest of the night.

I climb back into bed, close my eyes, and listen to the rain pelt the roof and splash into the water below.

Today was absolutely exhausting. But even so, it ended as a memorable day. A good day. And maybe tomorrow will be even better.

Chapter 7

Having lived with so many families, I've learned how different people come and go.

You notice it at the first meeting. Some folks extend their hand, like a formal greeting. Others want to embrace you with a hug, like they knew you from before and haven't seen you in a long time. Others don't say a thing and instead treat you as if you were magically dropped in their care without a warning.

And I've had plenty of goodbyes too. Parents who shook my hand when we first met also shook my hand when I departed. And people who didn't say much when I arrived often didn't say anything when I left.

But the hug from Jada is something I have not felt before. It doesn't have a category I can place it in, or another instance I can compare it to. It sits by itself in a space I don't recognize, but I want to hold on to it as long as I can.

I immediately think of it when I wake up, but I am

quickly distracted and surprised to see the light in the loft still on. Usually, Niko turns the generator off just after dinner to save gas throughout the night, and to make sure the lighted windows don't attract looters or thieves to the house while we are sleeping. He restarts it after breakfast, when we need the electricity to finish chores for the afternoon.

But we have not had breakfast yet, so something must be wrong.

To make matters worse, my towel trick didn't work, and the ceiling has been dripping all night. My pajamas are heavy with water and cling to my skin. Maybe that's why the loft feels colder today.

Shivering, I roll over and dig under the side table next to my mattress. I pull out another plastic bag with clothes inside to see if there's anything warmer than yesterday's outfit.

It's nearly impossible to keep anything dry up here, and most of the clothes I brought with me to Niko and Jada's are soaked through now, so I've been making do with the clothes Jada set aside for me.

When I open the bag, I find an outfit similar to the one she was wearing yesterday: cargo pants that are probably too big for me, a gray long-sleeve shirt, a plain sweatshirt, a sports bra, and some socks.

Guess I'm not changing underwear today.

I quickly put on the clothes and assess the rest of the loft. There are a couple places on the floor where small puddles have formed, and the cardboard box I threw my hatchet into also seems to be near a leak, because the top has bent over itself like a soggy sheet of paper.

I decide I'd better get the hatchet before Niko notices I don't have it on me. He hates when I don't pass the EDC check at breakfast, even though I think it's weird to have a sharp weapon on my hip so early in the morning. I head back to my mattress and grab my flashlight, lighter, and multitool, then grudgingly shuffle over to the box so that I can retrieve my hatchet.

As I'm about to grab it, however, two mice jump out of the top of the box. One runs up my wrist before leaping off, and the other hits the floor, back first, before flipping over and scurrying away. I let out a strangled gasp and frantically swipe at my arms, my neck, my legs—anywhere they could have touched.

"Stupid mice!" I yell as I dig in the box for my hatchet. "I thought we got rid of you already!"

I grab the handle, yank the hatchet out, and spin around to find out if I'm lucky enough to see where the mice hide next.

I scan my bed first. The last thing I want is a surprise guest when I am getting into bed later. The thought alone makes my skin crawl.

I throw the covers off, fully expecting a family of mice to flood out.

Thankfully, they've chosen somewhere else to hide.

"Niko! Jada! There's mice!" I announce as I walk across the loft, down the stairs, and into the make-shift kitchen. "Do we have any traps?"

No one responds.

The rain hitting the roof doesn't seem as loud as yesterday. Still, it's impossible to hear anyone unless you are in the same room or close to it, so I place the hatchet in its sheath on my waistband and head down the west hallway.

But that isn't a great move either. My first step in the hallway is met with soaking wet carpet.

"Ugh, are you serious?" I say to myself, lifting my foot to check the bottom.

Niko warned me about this last week when he said the wood and drywall would begin to absorb water from the first floor and bring it up here, to the second. He called it "capillary action." Jada called it "unlikely."

I call it "just another thing I wish Niko wasn't right about."

Even though the floor is drenched, I leave my boots behind. I don't want to waste another second getting to Jada. For the first time since the rain came, last night felt like more than just survival. It felt like what I think a family is supposed to feel like, and I want to experience it again. So I continue down the hallway, leaving dark footprints in the plush, damp carpet as I look to see where Niko and Jada are.

The first two Bin Room doors are open, but the

rooms are empty. We moved the food out of them weeks ago when we noticed mold growing in the corners and couldn't get it to stop, so now the only Bin Room left is in the east hallway.

I pass two more doors, to the bathroom and library, which are also open.

"Niko?! Jada?!" I shout, approaching each room.

Nothing.

I get all the way to the end of the hallway and see the staircase. We typically only go down here once a day to see how high the water is on the first level. We measure the height of the water in steps: Yesterday, it was six steps up. Today, it is considerably higher. It's almost to step eight, with only two more steps before it is fully on the second level.

This is not good.

The water has risen almost a full foot in less than a day. I'm sure Niko is already on the ham radio this morning, trying to learn any information he can.

I pass back through the living room across from the makeshift kitchen, and that's when I notice that all three Bug-Out-Backpacks are gone. Jada is probably going through them in the other hallway to make sure they are fully stocked, which means *I'll* have to triple-check them, again.

Another chore to help the day go by faster, I suppose.

I turn and get to the east hallway, and that's when I notice something I have not seen before. The door at the end of the hallway on the right, the INCH Room's door, is open.

Wide open.

The sight makes me stop in my tracks.

I can't explain why, but I have an uneasy feeling.

My breath quickens as I go from standing still to a full-out run, sending water splashing from the carpet onto the walls of the hallway.

"Niko? Jada? Niko? Jada?" I screech. "NIKO?! JADA?!"

No response.

No response.

No response.

Each door I pass is open, with no sign of Jada or Niko, and I can feel my chest grow tighter and tighter with each step until I reach the INCH Room.

"Niko? Jada?"

They must be here.

They have to be here!

There is nowhere else to go!

But when I get to the doorframe, I realize there must have been someplace to go.

Because Niko and Jada are gone.

Chapter 8

The INCH Room's open window is the first clear sign they have left. I'm not allowed to open a window unless Niko instructs me to do so. And it's clear why. There's water already pooling on the carpet.

The second sign is the rope ladder, which is bolted underneath the windowsill and draped over the edge outside. Its bright neon cords make it easy to spot through the dim light of the single bulb dangling from the center of the room.

And the third sign is the complete chaos everywhere.

Papers are scattered like small leaf piles; chairs are overturned as if someone had been grabbed mid-sentence. The desk drawers hang open, their contents dumped out in frantic handfuls.

My breath gets heavier. Slower.

This is not just a mess. These are signs of a *struggle*.

Or a quick departure.

My feet squish across the carpeted floor between the mess of papers as I go to see what is on the other side of the open window. It smells putrid, like something out of my worst nightmares.

But I have to fight the stench. I push my head outside into the pouring rain. Could Niko and Jada have fallen out? Were they right on the other side of the window?

But there is nothing noticeable except the rope ladder floating in the current as water rushes past the side of the house.

There is no boat. No escape path.

There is just black water.

I pull my head back in and feel the isolation of the single room push into me.

I am alone.

My hands shake as I shut the window to stop the rain from getting me wet, even though my head is already dripping with water and soaking my shirt. I try to slow my breathing, but my mind is spinning.

Where are they?

Where did they go?

Are they okay?!

What did I miss?!?

My head feels heavy, and I realize I am swaying in small circles, so I sit down before I collapse. I draw deep breaths to try to regain my composure, and take my first real look around the room.

Every other room in the house has a clear purpose: storage areas for food, extra clothing, supplies for BOB bags. But the INCH Room is different. Two identical desks are on either side, one with a radio system I don't recognize, and the other covered with books and loose paper, including multiple maps. Against the far side of the desk with the maps are three of the blue barrels I helped Jada move yesterday, a couple pairs of new-looking boots, and . . . my BOB from the living room? It's the only one that's dark green.

Why would they move it to the INCH Room without telling me?

I continue to scan the room for any sign, any clue, of what might have happened. The only thing that stands out is one of the maps. It has red markings on it and is placed directly next to another radio.

Stand up! I tell myself. *Just stand up!*

I get to my feet and move closer to see the map.

At first glance, I don't understand it at all. There are many shaky black circles with waves of green, orange, and blue overlayed on them, and it looks almost like ripples in water. There are no city names, no borders for states, and no key at the bottom. But there is something else. Red ink.

I put my finger on a red mark and trace it. It starts in the top right-hand corner of the map and weaves its way around the edges of the rippled, colored bands until it reaches an area where all the lines are pushed tightly together.

There, written and circled in red, are two words: *The Hill.*

I look at the rain-streaked window, then back at the map.

That's what the voice was talking about on Niko's ham radio. The Hill!

My mind races, trying to put together pieces of a puzzle I never knew about.

Is this what Jada wanted to tell me? Why didn't they tell me sooner? If I had known, maybe I could have helped them, whatever happened to them . . .

I move my finger off the map and look down at some of the stacked books on the desk. One is called *The Small Survivalist's Guide*, which I recognize immediately because Niko typically had it tucked away in his back pocket. This one doesn't have all the creases and folds in it, though, which means it's a backup. A different copy.

I suppose I shouldn't be surprised.

The single light in the room flickers on and off.

The genny!

It must be running out of gas, which means the lights won't be on much longer. I put my hand in my side pocket to feel the flashlight, just to be sure I have it. Then I pause for a moment as the flickering continues.

Finally, the flickering stops and the light stays on, so I move my hand off the flashlight and to the top book. I push it aside and look at the one underneath it, a green hardcover that reads *A Prepper's Guide to Worst-Case Scenarios*. There are a bunch of half-torn sticky notes poking out of the pages, so I flip open to the first one. It's stuck to a chapter heading called "BOB Crafting: The Essentials."

I flip to the next one.

"Generators: Electricity When You Need It."

I continue to check each marked page to see if anything offers some insight, but the chapters seem to cover things I already know about because of Niko and Jada's training.

"Rationing: How to Make Food Last."

"Security: Keep Your Dwelling Safe."

"Radios: Establishing Connections with Others."

I flip to the last marked page, and the title makes me pause.

"INCH: The Final Prep."

My eyes scan through the first paragraph.

> In your final phrase of prep work, establish an area, preferably a room with multiple points of entrance, as your INCH room (also known as "I'm Never Coming Home"). This will contain the final materials you will need before you depart your dwelling. First, stock it with enough food to last for at least . . .

I am reading the pages, but my mind is working simultaneously to try and make sense of what is happening.

I'm Never Coming Home.

I feel sick.

This can't be happening. They must have been taken, right? They wouldn't leave me here, would they?!

I put a hand on the desk to steady myself as a wave of nausea hits me.

SMASH!

The sudden sound of shattering glass overtakes the rain pounding on the roof and shocks my system. I close my eyes to assess whether this is real or just in my mind.

SMASH!

I hear it again, this time louder than the first.

I move my shaking hand from the desk to the wall to steady myself as I head out to look into the hallway.

The sound of breaking glass continues.

SMASH! SMASH! SMASH!

The lights flicker and then shut off, so I grab my flashlight and point the beam at the floor to guide me past the storage room doors while I stagger down the hallway. The beam of light shakes as my strength slowly begins to return.

I pause anyway, taking a moment to recover.

Breathe. Just breathe.

I pick my head up and walk until I reach the end of the hallway and round the corner to look at the living room.

But I can't see all that well, so I use the flashlight to scan the room until it hits something that instantly makes me cover my mouth to stop from screaming.

There is a man.

A man in a dark raincoat holding a large iron pipe, and he's hitting the remaining shards attached to the frame of the sliding-glass door.

There is another person already inside, too, rummaging through a bag.

The sudden yellow light on their faces gets their attention, and one of them yells in a deep, harsh voice:

"Grab her!"

Chapter 9

The first man crashes through the rest of the broken glass on the ground.

I pivot and run down the hallway, back to the INCH Room.

I know I am moving fast, but it doesn't feel like it—my feet slip on the wet carpet with each stride I take. The hallway lights flicker back on when I reach the INCH Room's door and slam it shut behind me.

I can feel the weight of the men's footsteps vibrating the floor as they stampede down the hall while I frantically try and lock the door with the deadbolt.

The moment I twist it shut, the door bends toward me as the men slam their bodies into it.

Is this what happened to Niko and Jada?

Who are these people?!

"Hit it with the pipe!" one yells.

The noise of the metal pipe's clanging—as it hits the door handle, again and again—rips through the small room. I can't take my eyes off the door. I walk backward.

Please don't open! Please hold!

I trip over something. It's a pair of Jada's old boots, sitting next to a blue barrel.

The barrels . . .

They float!

There is no more thinking now, just action. I slide my feet into the boots and drag an empty barrel over to the window.

"Give me that thing!" a voice yells. "I'll do it!"

The banging stops temporarily, and then resumes, harder this time.

I don't have much time!

I open the window as high as I can, lift the top of the barrel onto the ledge of the window, and heave it over, sending it splashing into the water below.

I turn around to face the door. The handle is crooked and shakes each time it is hit.

I need to leave!

I race over to the desk and focus on the map of The Hill.

This must have been their plan. This is the only option!

I rip the map off the corkboard and shove it into the small, zippered pocket of my backpack. As I lift the backpack to my shoulder, I catch a glimpse of a second hatchet, propped against another barrel.

Jada's voice comes into my head as I grab it.

"Two is one, one is none."

Before I can put it in my bag, though, the door bursts open. Both men stand there. Their chests heave up and down as they catch their breath, and water slides off their jackets onto the floor. The man on the right has a shaved head and a thick brown beard that covers his neck. To his left is the taller of the two, the man with the dark raincoat, who is pointing the metal pipe in my direction.

"Don't move, or this will not end well," he threatens.

I slowly pull my backpack over my left shoulder while tightly gripping the handle of the hatchet.

"I said, *don't move!*" he yells again.

"She's a kid," the other says, just audible enough. "She's got nothin'."

I raise the hatchet high above my head, hoping the sight of it will make them think twice. But I've never thrown it at anything other than the beam, and I can already feel my confidence plummeting.

So, I fake it.

"Don't . . . Don't come any closer!" My voice wavers. "Or I'll do it! I swear!"

"You won't," the bearded man confidently says. "You don't have it in you."

How does he know?

He puts his hand behind his back, then brings it back into view. He's holding a small gun that has speckles of brown and orange rust on its black frame.

"Like he said," the man adds, lifting the gun so it's eye level with me, "don't move."

A gun . . .

Niko said guns won't fire because of all the water and rust. So it can't shoot, right?!

"Put that thing down or I'll do it," he says, struggling to pull back the trigger back. "I will!"

It can't shoot! I have to believe it can't shoot!

The man pushes the gun farther forward, and I instinctively move backward until I feel my back hit the windowsill.

The lights flicker again, faster this time, which makes both men look up at the single lightbulb between us.

This is my chance. I have to throw it now!

I plant my left foot in front of me to hurl the hatchet in their direction, but my body freezes with fear.

I can't—I can't do it.

The small pause gives the man enough of a moment to make his decision. He extends his arm and pulls the trigger.

I hear the click, and I close my eyes, waiting for the inevitable pain of the bullet.

But it doesn't come.

"Eurgh!" the man yells, slamming the gun against his leg. "Get her!"

Panic overtakes me. The hatchet slips from my hand to the floor as I twist to the window. Gripping the frame, I launch myself out, hanging in the air for just a second before my body fully submerges in the cold water. My head goes down underneath the surface, but then the buoyancy of the backpack pulls me right back up into the onslaught of rain and water.

The first thing I spot is the blue barrel to my right, floating just a few feet away. Above me, the men's screams echo through the air, but I don't dare look up. Instead, I focus on kicking my legs and paddling my arms, fighting against the drag of my soaked clothes and heavy boots. Every movement feels sluggish as my limbs grow heavier with each stroke—but I'm close!

Faster! Faster!

I swing my arm up one more time and grasp the topside of the barrel just as I float around the corner of the house. The current is picking up, and the rain is splashing into the water so hard I can barely see where I am going; I can only focus on trying to get one arm next to the other before the barrel slips out from beneath me.

My feet snag on something, which spins me around to face the house as the current drags me backward. I can barely see the lights of the house—orange and yellow glows obscured by the lines of vertical rain—and within a matter of seconds they disappear as I drift farther and farther from the house and out toward the giant swirl of debris in the center of the street.

The current begins to weaken, and at the same time, the downpour of rain backs off to a steady fall, almost like the river and rain are coordinating their plans. The neighborhood around me is coming into view, but my focus is on the object in the middle of the debris swirl.

It's the aluminum boat! The one the man was trying to get in yesterday!

The barrel and I join the slow swirl and circle the dented boat along with the rest of the waste. I struggle to maintain my head above water as my body gets pushed around by the large mass of filth surrounding me. It's a dense tangle of broken wood, sticks, and cords, laced with the unmistakable stench of dead animals. The crunching and snapping of debris colliding around me makes me feel as if I'm breaking apart too. My strength is fading, and the boat, even though it's so close, feels impossibly out of reach.

"There! She's over there!" I hear a voice bark from behind me.

As the swirl rotates me, I face the direction I think the voice is coming from. Since the rain has thinned a bit, I can see the front of the mansion in the distance now. One man is standing in a window, likely still holding his weapon, and the other is climbing into a canoe.

I abandon my barrel and try to swim through the debris toward the boat. My legs aren't able to kick at all with so much surrounding me, so my only choice is to continue to pull myself through. It hurts each time I press my arms through the mess, and I can feel blades slicing into my arm from the shards of broken materials.

"The boat! She's headed for the boat!" I hear a voice yell again, but I don't turn around.

Focus! Faster!

I swing my arm high above the debris and latch on to whatever my hand can grasp to pull myself through the water. I get a solid hold on something and grab it with my other arm to pull myself across it. When my face gets in line with my hands, I see what it is.

It's a dead deer.

Its wet fur brushes against my chin as the animal sinks under the surface beneath my weight, vanishing into the murky water.

I have no time to panic now. I gasp for breath, my arms trembling as I scramble onto a partially submerged furniture cushion. It dips under my weight but holds just enough to keep me afloat. With one final reach, I grip the top edge of the boat and begin to pull myself in as the boat slowly tips toward me, nearly capsizing in my face.

"Hurry! She's almost in the boat!" I hear behind me.

I let out a scream and swing one leg over the tipping rim of the hull. The momentum slams the bottom of the boat back to the water and I land into the standing water in the boat.

The unexpected force of the fall sends liquid up

my nose, and I swallow a large mouthful of it. My body pulses from the surprising lack of oxygen, and I instinctively try to stand. Before I can, however, my stomach tries to reject its new contents, and I cough violently as my chest burns from the sudden influx of water in my lungs.

Don't stop! I tell myself. *I have to keep moving.*

I struggle to my knees, each breath rattling with the force of my coughs. My vision blurs for a moment before I manage to focus on the men. They're only a few boat lengths away now, closing the distance fast. The man in front paddles furiously, churning the water with each stroke, while the one in the back remains still, his unwavering gaze locked on to me.

I scan my boat for an oar or paddle, but instead of those, I see something better:

A motor!

I have never started or driven a boat, but I have seen enough movies in the foster care facility to know you need to pull the cord multiple times, like a lawnmower.

It must be the adrenaline in me, and because the boat is swirling, it shouldn't be possible, but I manage to grab each side of the boat and move to a standing position. The boat is spinning at a faster rate than the outside of the debris circle, and it sways unsteadily back and forth as I reach for the pull cord on the motor.

"*Stop!*" a voice yells.

The men have reached the edge of the circle and are cutting through it with the front of the canoe.

I grab the cord and give it the strongest pull I can.

It doesn't make a sound.

I pull it again. This time, a choke of mechanical noise.

Please start! Please! Please!

I give it a third pull and the engine spurts to life, spitting out dark smoke from the top right into my face.

The boat sluggishly moves as the men make their way deeper into the circle.

I rush to the front of the boat and recklessly stick my hands into the water, pushing aside all the debris that I can.

The boat surges forward, piercing its way directly through the debris as smoke continues to billow out of the motor.

Then I glance back at the men. They've stopped paddling, but their eyes remain fixed on me.

A shiver runs through me as I turn away, trying to focus on what lies ahead. The motor is running, and the current is directing the boat, weaving between the half-submerged houses of the neighborhood.

To where?

I have no idea.

But definitely not back.

Chapter 10

I haven't been to this part of the neighborhood until now, not even before the rain came. Jada and I made one trip in her giant SUV to a neighbor's house to drop off some paperwork, but other than that, I was either in the mansion or in the front yard. Nowhere else.

Miraculously, the rain has tapered off a tiny bit, making the view into the distance clearer than it's been all month. I can see the distant city skyline, but the tops of the buildings are hardly recognizable. The gray clouds and skyscrapers blend together, almost indistinguishable from one another. If it weren't for the windows occasionally catching the light seeping through breaks in the clouds, the horizon would seem like nothing more than an endless expanse of gray.

Adding to the gray is the smoke coming out of the sputtering boat's motor. I do not know how much gas is left, and I also don't know if the noise will attract more people.

But as long as I can't see the men behind me, I am safe for now.

I decide to press the red button on top to kill the engine. As I look around, the boat and I glide silently but swiftly above the water. That's when the reality of what has just taken place begins to sink in.

Niko and Jada left me in the middle of the night. They just *left* me.

But the thought of that doesn't make any sense to me. Niko taught me how to defend myself. Jada and I bonded. And how would they leave, anyway?! Niko and Jada don't have a boat.

Or do they?

I scan my surroundings again, as if my foster parents will suddenly appear.

Where did you go? Why did you leave me alone?

I look ahead to try and figure out where I am going, but it doesn't help. All I know is that I am still in a neighborhood. The houses around me are close together and varying in size, but they are all in the same condition: They are falling apart.

Some homes can only be seen because of the chimneys sticking up out of the water, and two-story structures are only slightly higher, with the second-floor windows exposed.

I take a quick glance over the edge of the boat into the water. It is a dark, thick, chocolatey brown, except for the chemicals that reside on top of it. Swirls of rainbow colors bend and overlap as the hull of my boat pushes through and sends them rotating off to the side. I can only imagine what is underneath: cars, bushes, bicycles, mailboxes, fences, all trapped under the moving slush of filth and debris—everything that the people in this neighborhood had owned.

That's where my belongings would be, too, if I had any.

I was never one to carry much with me from house to house besides some clothes I really liked, including a large, comfy sweatshirt I got from a University of Iowa basketball game that the foster care center took me and the other kids to. Everyone got the same sweatshirt after the game, and even though mine was two sizes too large, I grew into it. It carried a good memory I could think about when I wore it.

I wish I had it now. Was it even in one of the plastic bags under my side table, or was it lost to the old bedroom? Who could know anymore?

I pass another two-story home. The windows are all shattered, but overall this home seems in better shape than the others, and there are signs of people too. On top of the roof is a camping tent, but the sides of it have collapsed and are waving in the small gusts of wind. Next to the tent is a cooler and a patio chair, but they're rusted, and they don't look like they've been used in weeks.

How long did those people last? Where are they?

Did someone attack them too?

The current continues to guide me, pulling the boat to the backside of the house and around the top of a tree. After I pass the branches that dip in and out of the water, I take a look back at the house for more signs of life, but instead I see something else.

On the slope of the black-and-brown tiled roof are words spray-painted in white.

HELP! NEED FOOD!

We had food. We could have helped if we only knew.

The thought of last night's chicken makes my stomach knot. I haven't eaten since then.

I rescan the area to make sure the men are gone, then take my backpack off my shoulder and do a check of my EDC items. The hatchet and flashlight are still on me, but my multitool and lighter are missing. They must have fallen out in the struggle to get in the boat.

I suppose I am lucky to have anything at all.

I try to pull open the backpack, but my hands are stiff and can't grasp the zipper as my body shivers uncontrollably from the cold, wet clothes that cling to me.

If I don't get dry quick, I'm in trouble.

Each attempt at the zipper is more sluggish than the last, and my skin tightens with a biting cold that seems to crawl deeper with every movement. My fingers are almost completely numb now, and the zipper refuses to cooperate.

Come on! This should be easy!

I finally manage to pull the zipper up and assess

the contents of the bag. It's waterproof, or so they say, but the fabric is waterlogged. Still, there's a chance the inside is still dry.

I already know what *should* be in there: food, water, matches, another flashlight, and batteries, but that is not what I see first.

The first thing I see is a clear sealed bag, and it has clothes in it. Dry clothes.

Niko and Jada added more things to my backpack? Why?

What were they planning?

I lift the clothing bag up to see what other surprises might be underneath and discover a black cylinder, which I know contains a compressed rain jacket and pants.

I need to get these on now, before hypothermia sets in.

But there is no point in trying to change into dry clothes if I have to get them wet all over again. The boat floor is still filled with several inches of water, so I make emptying it the priority. Using just my hands, I slosh it over the side of the boat. Each plunge makes my fingers ache and stiffen, but I continue anyway.

I'm able to get the water level just below the soles of my boots, and then I rip open the plastic bag.

Cargo pants, long-sleeve shirt, socks, underwear, and . . .

My Iowa sweatshirt?!

Why is it here?

I quickly shed my wet clothes and put on the dry

ones. Then a fictional image of Jada carefully rolling the sweatshirt up and packing it forms in my brain. Before I put my boots back on, I tear the straps off the compressed rain gear, unroll the jacket and pants, and layer them over my clothes. Despite the dry cotton material on my skin, I am still shivering, but at least it seems contained.

When I finally sit down on the single bench in the aluminum boat, I'm able to take in my surroundings again. The water is so wide and vast, it almost seems like the houses rained down into the water rather than the other way around. I am still moving forward at a good speed without the motor, and with no signs of trouble ahead, I dig into the backpack once more.

The things I expected to be there are in order, but there are extra things as well: a small water-purifying straw, a single flare stick, and some more matches.

Better than nothing.

I zip the bag shut and open the small pouch to reveal the map from the INCH Room. I am not sure how much it will help me since I do not know where I am, but I unfold it anyway. I spot the messily written phrase in red at the top of the map and suck in a breath.

The Hill.

I think to myself, *Niko and Jada were taken, right? They wouldn't have just left me.*

The thought grips me, cold and unwelcome.

Which one is better? Them having abandoned me on purpose or taken by another force unwillingly?

I can't decide which hurts less.

What if they were taken?

Dragged from the house in the middle of the night while I slept just a few feet away?

The image flashes behind my eyes—Jada struggling, Niko shouting through a cloth meant to silence him, a window left open.

Or maybe something worse.

I swallow hard, pressing my fingers against the paper as if holding it tighter will keep the panic from setting in. I shake my head, trying to chase away the spiraling thoughts, but the other possibilities are already rooting deep.

What if they left on purpose?

My breath comes too fast, too sharp. I need to move. Sitting here, thinking, guessing—it won't help. I have to do *something.*

I look again at the red marks, as if doing it another time will help uncover a locked clue, but it doesn't. The map is just as confusing as it was when I found it, and the circled words stand out like they are teasing me.

The Hill.

I pick my head up and look around to see if anything will help me interpret the map. The rain is beginning to pick up again, and I can only see a few feet in front of me as I float down the middle of the flooded street.

Nothing else is visible.

Nothing else to help me figure out where I am, or where I may be going.

It is just me, the boat, and a map I can't read.

I am alone.

Chapter 11

I have gotten used to being by myself over the years.

The first family I remember living with had six kids already, all of whom were older than me. I was only seven when I joined them, and it was clear from the beginning that I was not welcome, probably because we all knew it was temporary. Even so, I still wanted to join them, no matter how poorly everyone treated me. But as hard as I tried to connect, the distance between me and the family stayed the same. I quickly learned that in order to have a chance to be happy, in order to accept my situation, I would also have to accept being alone.

Maybe that's why I never connected well with anyone. I have no space for them. But the situation I am in now is deeper than being alone, or wanting to be alone.

This is isolation.

After floating in the boat for hours, nothing has changed except that I seem to be leaving the neighborhoods filled with collapsing houses and entering a less populated area. There are occasional signs of fast-food restaurants sticking up out of the water like candles on top of a cake, but there are no traces of life anywhere. My best guess is I am floating over what was once a highway, or maybe a series of large farm fields. There isn't a whole lot out here; the benefit of that is I don't have to worry about the boat crashing into anything.

But it is also a negative.

I need a place to sleep and, more important, to get out of the rain.

Each drop of it explodes like tiny bullets, turning the surface of brown liquid into a roiling battlefield of ripples and waves. The sky doesn't look much different, either, as it swirls a looming mass of ash-colored clouds like it's about to collapse, and when that sky meets the horizon of the water, steam rises in a ghostly fog, shrouding the scene in an apocalyptic mist.

I decide my best bet is to maneuver on top of something, anything, that will allow me to anchor the boat securely for the night. I don't know how much gas is left in the engine, or if it will even turn on again, but if I see something worth exploring, I have to try.

After what seems like a few more hours of sitting hunched in the hull of the boat, still paranoid someone might be after me, the sky turns black, and I have to turn on my flashlight to navigate in the water. The beam of light doesn't travel far through the rain, but I can see buildings again, which might be my only chance to find shelter.

I scan back and forth with the light until I see a structure sticking considerably higher than the others out of the water, maybe ten to fifteen feet. As I get closer, I recognize what it is, and relief sets in.

It's a parking garage. A giant parking garage.

The concrete slabs become clearer as my light ricochets off the windshields of the cars inside. Everything seems like it hasn't moved in weeks, which means it might be a safe place to stay without the fear of it collapsing, at least for a while.

I grab the handle of the engine cord to give it a swift tug, but a sudden realization sets in.

People could be in there.

I grip the edges of the boat, my fingers pressing into the damp aluminum as I stare into the dark mouth of the flooded parking garage, where unseen figures might be waiting. They could be helpful, or they could be like the men who attacked me earlier.

It feels like a gamble I'm not sure I can afford to take.

I find myself wishing Niko or Jada were here. I wish someone were here to tell me what to do.

Another gust of rain pelts my face, and I feel my resolve cracking. If I don't find shelter soon, exhaustion will make the choice for me. I glance one more time into the dark, weighing the risk against the need.

I have to go in. I can't stay out here at night.

Before I change my mind, I yank on the pull cord of the motor. It starts right away. A small miracle in this disaster of a situation.

I navigate the boat as close as I can to the garage before cutting the engine again, and the vessel maintains its path and glides through the large opening between two half-submerged cars. There is still another floor above me and another above that, but as long as the ceiling is intact, this may be a viable place to stay dry and safe for the night.

I continue to trace the ceiling of the parking garage with the light until I see an exposed staircase with a metal rail. I hold the flashlight in my mouth and quickly stick my hands in the cold water to steer the boat. Once I am close enough, I grab the railing and guide the boat closer to the steps until I hear the scraping of the aluminum frame of the boat against the concrete.

The sound is unavoidable as it reverberates, and I pause for a response.

Nothing.

Without rocking the boat too much, I grab my soaking wet sweatshirt from the pile of old clothes and exit at the front of the now-docked boat. Using the sleeves, I tie one end of the sweatshirt to the rail and knot the other around the boat's handle, tugging each side to make sure it's secure.

I pause, and the boat doesn't move.

To be sure it won't float away, I grab the boat by the hull and pull as hard as I can to drag it up one more step.

CLANG!

The aluminum hitting the open steps echoes throughout the concrete structure, but I pull again. I must secure the boat.

CLANG! CLANG! CLANG!

With the boat now mostly out of the water, I grab my backpack and take the flashlight from my mouth, casting the beam of light up the stairwell.

The path upward is a mess of everything the flood has left behind—slick with algae, caked in mud, and littered with scraps of debris that have been carried in by the rising water.

Each step is a hazard, a patchwork of wet leaves, broken twigs, and unidentifiable sludge, all adding to the wretched smell of sewage that floods my nose. The metal railings are just as bad, coated in a thin film of rust-colored grime that drips, adding to the mess of every single stair. A wrong move here doesn't just mean a fall—it means slipping into the water, too, into whatever lurks beneath the surface.

I need to move carefully.

I need to make sure it's safe.

It is quieter here than it was in the mansion. Besides the sound of water sloshing against the cars and walls of the garage, I can't really hear the rain anymore, which is an odd sensation. After weeks of listening to it pelt the roof of the mansion, not hearing the rain makes it seem like I am missing something. It is a loud, almost deafening silence that makes my ears hum. The air feels heavier here, too, almost suffocating, with a musty stench that pushes up against my face as I climb the stairs.

Up on the last step now, I shine my light onto the next floor.

Yes! It is dry in here.

There are a few puddles between the abandoned cars, which are all parked perfectly between the white parking lines, but from what I can see, the garage is vacant. Still, I decide to stay crouched by the stairs, just in case.

As time goes by, I don't hear any other sounds, so I stand up and move to the maroon van just in front of me. All the doors are shut, which might be a safe place to sleep as long as it's unlocked and dry inside.

I put my hand on the door and pull the handle. It clicks, and I slide the door open. I'm lucky. Whoever was in the van must have been in a hurry to leave and didn't lock it.

Inside is something even luckier—something I did not expect to find. A bed. An actual bed. The back seats have been removed and in their place are blankets and two pillows.

But my relief turns to anguish when I see two small stuffed animals in the corner. One is a giraffe, and the other an elephant.

There were kids here. Children.

For the first time since entering the garage, I do not feel alone. Instead, I am suddenly surrounded by the haunting presence of hypothetical memories that are not mine. I see a happy family, full of love and life, sitting in the back of the van. Two parents snuggling with their kids, telling them that everything is going to be okay as they hold their stuffed-animal friends.

I can feel the tears coming, and my face tightens to prevent them from spilling out.

Still, I climb into the van, shut the door, and take off my rain gear, boots, and socks. I gently lift the two stuffed animals and hug them close as I pull the blankets over me and try to find comfort in a bed that was meant not for me but for someone else.

I sleep on and off the entire night. There are no nightmares, but each time I wake up, I think I am somewhere else:

In my bed at the mansion, before the rain came.

On the orange couch of my second foster home.

On the bottom bunk in the fourth home.

I have to remind myself that I am in the maroon van in the parking garage, and when I do, the anxiety in my heart rises, and I struggle to calm myself down in order to fall back asleep.

So this last time, I don't try.

I sit up and look through the van window to the ocean of filth outside the parking garage. The rain is slow, and there is a little more sunlight penetrating through the clouds now than yesterday, which means I might be able to better explore the area while conserving the battery in my flashlight. Before I leave, I open the backpack and find my first meal, a bag of instant breakfast skillet. The directions say I am supposed to add hot water, but since that is obviously not going to happen, I open one of the cold water bottles and dump it in the pouch. Stirring it doesn't make it any more appetizing, but at least it's something.

The first bite is horrible. It's a mixture attempting to be food, and it's disgusting. Still, I desperately need it.

I reluctantly choke the rest of the "skillet" down, put my socks and boots back on, and slowly open the van door to avoid making a sound. I can already see that the parking garage is not as small as it seemed in the dark, and there are more cars than I initially thought.

In fact, there is *a lot* more to look at.

Two clusters of folding chairs form circles between the rows of cars, each centered around a trash can. Nearby, a few logs rest on the ground next to some flattened, discarded boxes, like they are waiting to be used.

Am I in a camp? Could there be someone else here?!

A wave of fear tightens around my chest as I realize the potential danger I am in.

If others are here, who are they? And more important—do they know I'm here too?!

My fingers tighten around the handle of my hatchet as I lower myself into a crouch. Moving slowly, I slip behind the next car, pressing my back against the rusted frame and trying not to make a single sound.

I hold my breath, listening—waiting—each one of my muscles tensed, ready for whatever comes next . . .

Nothing.

I wait a few more minutes.

Nothing.

There isn't a sound, so I stealthily move behind the car to the next one.

Then the next.

And then another, until I am standing parallel to the first set of chairs and see something I haven't seen in months.

Birds. Dozens of them.

The small black birds are gathered in the opposite aisle, wedged between two trucks and standing wing to wing as if they are waiting for orders. If it weren't for the few that occasionally move their heads back and forth, I would think they were fake. I stand up to get a better look, and all the birds turn their heads in my direction.

"Don't worry, I'm not going to hurt you," I assure them as I walk forward to get a better view.

We all stare at each other for a moment, and then an abrupt clang echoes throughout the parking garage. The birds scatter beneath the trucks on either side, and I spin around to see what is behind me.

CLANG! CLANG! CLANG!

I put the hatchet back in the sheath and start running toward the stairs, because I know the sound.

It's the boat! It might have come untied! That's my only way out!

CLANG! CLANG! CLANG!

The sharp, metallic echoes ricochet off the concrete walls, each one louder than the last.

It's the boat. It has to be!

A surge of panic grips me as my boots slap against the puddles on the ground. If it's come untied, if the current is pulling it away, my only way out is drifting into the darkness.

My pulse slams into my ribs and my arms pump at my sides as I race past the abandoned van, and the stairs come into view, slick with rain and algae, but I don't slow down. Another *CLANG* rings out, the sound scraping against my nerves.

Please, please, please! Don't drift off!

I turn the corner into the stairwell and leap over the first few steps—but the moment my feet hit the slick pavement, they slip out from under me.

A jolt of pain explodes through my back as I

crash down, and my head whiplashes against the final step. It immediately takes my breath away. I stare up, blinking uncontrollably as a series of colors burst behind my eyes. For a moment, it feels like the ground beneath me is tilting, and each time I breathe, my vision gets smaller and smaller as a blanket of darkness takes over.

But before my eyes completely shut, something comes into frame.

The face of a . . . boy?

Chapter 12

Are you hurt?" the boys asks. "Are you okay?"

The back of my head throbs. I open my mouth to talk, but nothing comes out. The pain is overwhelming, and I can't focus my eyes for more than a second before they shut again.

"Oh no! You're bleeding!" the boy announces. "Don't move, I'll be right back!"

I hear his feet go up the steps, and then the sound is replaced by the boat rocking in the water and grinding against the steps. I try to turn my head to see if it's floating away, but my body is twitching uncontrollably.

I think I am in shock.

Minutes go by before the boy reappears in front of me.

"Umm, okay, let's try this," he says uncertainly. "I'm going to put this around your head."

He squats down as the blur in my eyes dissipates, and I can finally make out some details. He has sleek, jet-black hair, which falls in uneven clumps around his face. Each strand sticks out just enough to make it look effortlessly cool, like he didn't even have to try.

He lifts my head and wraps something around it. I'm not twitching anymore, but the pain at the back of my head is growing intensely.

"I think that will hold for now," he assures me. "Let's try and sit you up."

He wraps both his arms around me and drags me a few feet over until I am leaning against the wall of the staircase. I can see the boat now, which thankfully is still tied to the railing.

"My boat," I whisper. "Get it . . . get it on the steps."

"That's *your* boat?!" he exclaims. "Okay, I can try!"

I watch him struggle to get it up the steps as the clangs reverberate throughout the pillars of the garage. He doesn't seem weak, but his thin build and short appearance make me think he is much younger than I am.

He manages to dock the boat, then rejoins me on the steps.

I have so many questions for him, like:

Are there others?

How long have you been here?

Do you have food?

Are we in danger?!

Before I can ask anything, he starts with the answer to the question I should have asked first.

"My name is Kota," he says as he buttons the top of his jacket. "What's your name?"

As I breathe in to answer, the pain in my head launches into a sharp stab, and I close my mouth to try and bury it.

"Take your time," Kota consoles me, adjusting his position so he is in front of me. "You don't have to talk if you don't want to."

I give him the smallest nod, and he moves one of his hands to the top of my knee. The touch is comforting, and we sit in silence for a few minutes as the sharp pain slowly transitions into a manageable ache.

"I'm . . . Aurora," I finally answer him, minutes later, and then ask my first question. "Are there . . . others here?"

"There used to be," Kota says, leaning back against the wall. "I am the only one left, unless you count all the birds."

The water in front of us churns and splashes up the steps, hitting our feet.

"We should go," I suggest. "I need somewhere to lie down."

Kota doesn't respond but stands up first to help me. Together, the two of us ascend the slippery steps one at a time as he braces me with his hands. Once we are at the top, I point to the van, and he guides me to the door.

"I knew this family," Kota says despondently as he stares at the van. "I watched the kids sometimes during the adult meetings."

I want to know what happened to them, but there

is something in his voice that makes it seem like I shouldn't ask. So instead of responding, I grab the handle and open the door. Kota rushes to get in front of me and helps me down onto the bed of soft blankets, then adjusts the pillow until it fits comfortably under my neck.

"Thank you," I say again. "This is much better than the steps."

"I would offer you food, but I don't have any," he says. "I haven't eaten in two days."

"I have some food," I announce. "It's in my backpack."

Kota doesn't hesitate and unzips the backpack. He pulls out another instant meal bag—one he must be familiar with, since he immediately empties the last water bottle into it.

"Here, we can share it," Kota suggests, and brings the edge of the bag to my lips. "I think this is supposed to be warm oatmeal."

For some reason, that makes me chuckle, and he pulls the bag back to avoid spilling it. Once I stop, Kota tries again, and I get my first taste.

It's disgusting, just like the last one. But it is food.

Kota lifts it to his mouth next and takes a much longer sip, like the contents are his favorite meal in the entire world.

As we share the meal together, Kota explores the rest of my backpack until he pulls out the map.

"What's this?" he asks, unfolding the map and

laying it across my legs for both of us to see. "Why do you have a topography map?"

"Is that what it is? A topography map?" I ask, massaging the top of my head. "I can't read it."

"Oh, well, I can," Kota says nonchalantly. "We used these in Scouts all the time. It shows elevation changes and other features of an area."

This gets my attention, and I tap the map with my finger.

"Do you know how to get here?" I ask, pointing to the red circle labeled *The Hill.*

"Um . . . I would have to know where we are first," he says, rotating the map. "But I think I might be able to figure it out, as long as this is a map of *here*."

I didn't even think about that. The map could be a completely different city or state. But if Niko and Jada were making plans to go there, then it has to be close, right? How far can you get when the whole world is flooded?

"What do you need?" I ask as I try to sit up. "What do you need to read the map?"

"I'd need a compass," Kota starts. "But I have one already, see?"

Kota pushes his arm in front of my face and points to the small yellow compass built into the cuff of his jacket. It's about the size of a quarter.

"My dad got this jacket for me when I joined Scouts last year," he says, pulling his arm back and looking at the compass. "It's my . . ."

Kota's voice cracks, and he stops himself before he loses himself to it, then starts over. "It's my . . . favorite jacket."

I unzip the shell of my rain jacket and point to the Hawkeye symbol in the middle of my University of Iowa sweatshirt.

"I have a favorite too," I say, trying to comfort him. "Mine doesn't have a compass, though, but it does have some holes."

The small joke makes Kota smile as he stares at my sweatshirt and then back at his compass. His gaze is distant, like he is reliving a painful moment, and although I want to ask him about it, I also want to stay focused on forming our plan, at least for now.

There is a long pause before he continues.

"The hardest part will be figuring out where we are," he says as I zip up my jacket. "With everything flooded, it's hard to see the other places on the map, like rivers and valleys." Another pause.

"Why do you want to go there?" Kota asks, pushing the map closer to me again and tapping the red lettering. "What is *The Hill*?"

"I'm not sure," I admit. "But I think it might be a safe place to go."

"Well, I know why it has that name," Kota says confidently. "See how all the lines are close together? That means it's the highest place on the map."

The highest place? A place away from the rising water?

Is that where Niko and Jada were planning to go? Could they possibly be there?

If Kota is telling the truth, then there doesn't seem to be any other option. He doesn't have any food, I barely have any, and I also don't know how to read the map. We are both going to have to leave the parking garage at some point.

The question is, am I going to do it alone, or are we going to do it together?

I have limited supplies, a gash on my head, and a boat. But for some reason I can't explain, that still seems like enough to be able to help someone else, especially another kid.

"I think we should go together," I tell Kota, as I try to lock eyes with him to gauge his reaction. "I think we can make it out of here."

Kota must have been hoping for the same thing, because his eyes light up. But just as I am about to tell him the rest of the plan forming in my head, they dim again.

"We can't leave," he says firmly as he folds the map back up. "It's impossible."

"Why?" I ask. "We can at least try."

Kota looks out the open van door toward the moving water just beyond the barrier of the garage.

"The Dark Pools are out there," he says, extending his hand toward the water.

I look out to the water, expecting to see something I might have missed when I first entered the parking garage, but all I see is the same ocean of filth as before.

"I don't understand," I say, trying to follow the direction of his hand. "What are Dark Pools?"

Kota looks back at me, his eyes now full of tears.

"They're what killed everyone else."

Chapter 13

Kota sits back and puts his arms around his knees, pulling them tight to his chest. The position makes him seem even younger than he is, especially with the stuffed elephant and giraffe sitting next to him.

I need more information, but I also don't want to upset Kota any more than he seems to be, so I choose my next words carefully.

"How long have you been on your own, Kota?" I ask gently.

Kota grabs the elephant, bringing it just in front of his knees.

"It feels like a long time, but I'm not sure. Maybe a couple weeks. I've been living in a van on the other side of the garage."

He strokes the top of the elephant's head, then carefully places it back next to the giraffe.

"There were four families here in the garage, including mine," he starts, his eyes dropping to the floor of the van. "We were lucky enough to have a boat and two small canoes here, enough for all of us to leave. I didn't want to. None of us did. But we were running out of food, so we had to try."

Kota takes a deep breath, like he is steadying himself for whatever he is going to say next.

"One family—a mom, a dad, and their two sons—they left first," Kota starts. "They only got a little way out before they vanished into a Dark Pool. A few days later, two other families shared a boat and left, and we watched the same thing happen to them. The Dark Pool just took them away."

"I'm so sorry," I say, trying to console him with the little energy I have. "I still don't understand what you are saying, though. What is a Dark Pool?"

Kota looks at me, his eyebrows forming downward slopes over his eyes. "You . . . you haven't seen one? Out on the water?"

"I might have," I say. "But I don't know what they look like."

Kota crawls over to me and leans against the side of the van.

"It's a black circle on the water," he says while tracing an imaginary circle in the air. "So dark I can't really describe it. Like a deep, deep hole that never ends."

"But what are they?" I ask again. "They can't be holes. That doesn't make sense."

Kota stops making the circle and looks back out the van door.

"My grandma said it's the souls of the dead, the shui gui, coming up from the flooded graves below."

I'm surprised to hear Kota speak in a different language.

"What is *shu* . . . What did you say?" I ask.

"Shui gui," Kota repeats. "Water ghosts."

I have never believed in ghosts, but the serious look in Kota's eyes says he does.

"I know it sounds made up," he admits before I can say anything else. "The other adults thought they were just giant bubbles of gas coming up from the earth, but I believe Grandma. I saw one too."

"Wait. You *saw* a water ghost?" I ask.

"No, but I saw the Dark Pool. My baba, my grandma, and I tried to leave in the last canoe. We got farther than the others, but when our canoe started to tip forward, Baba grabbed me and threw me as far as he could into the water. When I looked back, the Dark Pool was shrinking—and they were both gone."

"So you swam back here?" I guess.

Kota nods. "That's why we can't leave. The Dark Pools are everywhere. The shui gui are waiting."

There is a lull for a moment while I try to absorb everything he's said. Although I don't believe in the water ghosts, I do believe Kota's fear. People disappearing into the water without any explanation would make me just as scared. But how come that didn't happen to me when I was on the water? Or when the men were chasing me? Why haven't I seen a Dark Pool?

"I am so sorry about your family, Kota," I say. "I can't imagine what you've been through."

Kota taps the compass on his sleeve, and the quiet lingers between us for a moment.

"Do you have a family?" he asks, breaking the silence.

The easiest—and most complicated—answer to that question is *I don't know.*

There's no history of my birth parents that I can give. My case file exists—or rather, existed—but like my memory, it's empty of anything that resembles a real family. Maybe I once knew their names, but if I did, they're long gone.

I don't know who they were. I don't know where I came from.

I am from nothing.

And maybe that's why I want to help Kota.

Anything, or anyone, is better than nothing. Right?

Instead of telling Kota all that, however, or about my foster families, or Niko and Jada, I decide to tell him something else.

A bended truth.

"They are no longer here, and that's all there is to say," I respond, then quickly change the subject back to the original plan: leaving. "I don't question what you saw out there, Kota, but we don't have a choice, and I think you know that. There is no way we can survive in here. We need to leave. We *can* leave. We have a map. An actual map that could help us get somewhere, and you—you can read it," I encourage.

“I don’t know,” Kota says. “What if I *can’t* actually read the map?”

“I believe you can,” I say with as much confidence as I can muster. “I need you to try.”

Kota looks down at his compass and shifts his weight. “You really think I can?”

“I *know* you can,” I continue, and put my hand on the back of my head. “And I think if I just rest for another day or two, I’ll be ready too.”

“Okay, let’s do it,” Kota agrees. “Let’s get to The Hill together.”

Chapter 14

We do not have much time left in the parking garage. With only enough food to last us another couple of days, the sooner we can leave, the better.

But I am not better, not yet.

While I rest in the van and let my head heal, Kota rummages through the other vehicles to see if he can find anything that will help us in our journey. Every once in a while, he comes back to show me what he's found.

"What about this?" he suggests enthusiastically. "Maybe we can use it to paddle?"

Kota is holding a small shovel he found in the back of a pickup truck. It's not the best choice, but we also don't have anything else to help move the boat if the motor runs out of gas.

"Good find," I tell him. "Why don't you put it in the pile of other stuff?"

"You got it," Kota says almost cheerfully as he leaves to place it just behind the van, where we have accumulated the other things, like:

- Five feet of thick nylon rope. This will come in handy if we need to tie up the boat.
- A blue tarp, about as big as the boat. This will help keep the rain off us while we travel, and hopefully keep rain out of the boat.
- Two extra blankets from the van. The temperature seems to still be decreasing, and we don't have any extra clean clothes.

It isn't much, but my confidence about leaving the garage increases with each object Kota finds.

As he goes off for another round of material hunting, I tend to my head.

I remove the white cloth that Kota wrapped around me earlier. It's not white anymore because the blood from the wound has dyed most of it a soft pink color. After tossing the fabric to the side, I push my hand through my hair to where the pain is coming from and feel the cut on the back of my head.

It doesn't seem deep, but it is pretty long, maybe two or three inches. I reach into my BOB and open the IFAK to find exactly what I am looking for: butterfly bandages.

Normally, any sort of sticky bandage won't work when long hair is involved, but I don't have much of a choice, and the cloth is too soiled now to use. I take the hatchet off my hip and hold it out behind my head while I grasp the hair around the cut with my other hand.

Moving in a back-and-forth motion like a saw, I use the hatchet to cut the hair as close to my head as possible to give the butterfly bandages the best chance to stick. With the small chunk of hair gone, I delicately remove the plastic from the bandages and place each one over the cut, squeezing the sides of the wound to help secure the bandage as close as possible. It's not the best hair trim or wound covering, but if Jada hadn't forced me to learn about the IFAK, it would be a lot worse.

"I know it's gross to think about," Jada had admitted in one training session, during the second week of rain, "but if one of us gets hurt, we need to be able to help each other."

"I'm not sure I am much help to anyone," I said as I fumbled with the gauze and bandage in my hand. "I've never really been that good at anything."

"I highly doubt that," Jada laughed, a noticeable change in demeanor from the onslaught of new responsibilities and pressure from the rising water. "Niko told me you hit the beam with the hatchet ten times in a row yesterday. I'd say that's pretty good!"

"Thanks." I smiled, taking in the warmth of the compliment. "I think Niko is just glad I didn't hit the window like last time."

"I heard that!" Niko bellowed from around the corner. "Maybe I'll just have you practice with a shoe from now on."

The three of us laughed together as I continued

to mess up the layout of the gauze. What I wouldn't give to laugh with them now . . .

"Whoa! You cut that patch of hair off yourself? That's impressive!" Kota announces, pulling me back from the memory as he reappears from around the door of the van. "We should keep the strands you cut off, though. Can I see them?"

"Are you serious?" I ask, picking up the clumps of hair from the floor of the van. "Why would we want my hair?"

"Well," Kota starts, "I've only done it a couple times in Scouts, but with long hair you can make flies for fishing, if you have a fishing pole and hook."

"Do you have a fishing pole?" I ask.

Kota shakes his head.

"Do you have a hook?" I continue, handing him the hair.

"No." Kota pauses. "But we do have a bunch of soda cans lying around. I can use the pop tops to make hooks!"

Before I can say anything, Kota disappears back into the parking garage, and I can hear the cans clattering around and echoing as he picks them up. He returns with an armful of cans and brings them into the van.

We spend the rest of the afternoon and evening sitting and talking while Kota makes flies. It's really impressive, and so far, this is the most confidence I have seen from him. After breaking off the pop top of the can, he snaps it in half to form a sharp hook. Then, he wraps strands of hair around it several times until it begins to look like a fuzzy bug.

By the time we finish sharing another bag of instant cold oatmeal with some leftover clean water that we found in the van, Kota has finished making seven flies in the hopes we will actually have a chance to fish.

With his hands and brain less occupied now, we begin making our plan for the following morning.

"I am not sure how much gas is left in the motor," I tell Kota as I open the backpack. "But I think it's our best bet for getting past Dark Pools if they show up."

"I hope so," Kota agrees, putting the newly made flies into the small zipper pouch of the backpack. "I'm nervous."

"Me too," I admit. "Me too."

When we wake up the next morning, however, I don't have a desire to move. Kota and I are lying next to each other in the back of the van, and for a second, it just seems like we are two kids on a fun family adventure, without a care in the world except what treat we are going to get at the next gas station.

I am guessing Kota feels the same way. He is holding the elephant again, so I offer one last suggestion before we leave.

"We could take that with us," I offer. "There's room in the boat, if you want."

Kota takes the elephant and the giraffe, places them against his pillow, and covers them with the edge of the blanket.

"Thanks, Aurora. But I want them to stay here, together," he says as he tucks the blanket tightly around them. "It's where they should be."

I smile at Kota and then slowly sit up to feel the back of my head. The butterfly bandages held throughout the night, and even though it still hurts to touch, I don't feel the dizziness I felt the day before.

I slide my rain jacket over my sweatshirt as Kota pulls his yellow poncho over his Scouts jacket, and we gather our supplies and make our way down to the boat.

When we reach the stairs, I have to step over my bloodstain from the day before, and it instantly makes me nauseous. I catch myself on the railing to steady my stomach, then look out of the small opening in the concrete wall to take in the dark water outside. It's the calmest I've seen the water in days, and I can see the faint glittering of mist above the vast horizon of water. This could be the best opportunity to see some sort of landmark that can help Kota interpret the map.

"I'll get in first so I can be in the back and work the motor," I say as I step down two more steps and into the wobbling boat, which is still half out of the water. "You can be in the front to be our eyes, okay?"

I turn around to help Kota in, but he has stepped back farther away from the boat.

"Hey, we can do this," I encourage, and reach out my hand. "I know we can."

Kota shuffles his feet for a moment, then takes my hand, and I help him find a good place to sit at the bow of the boat.

"Go ahead and untie it," I instruct Kota, pointing at my old sweatshirt anchoring the boat. "I'll use the shovel to steer until we get out of the garage and into open water."

Once Kota manages to free the boat, he reaches into my backpack and pulls out the flashlight. It isn't too dark in the garage, and I can see where I need to go, but when he clicks on the light, I get a weird sense of relief, like we are somehow safer with it on.

With Kota now acting as a spotlight, I use the shovel to push away from the staircase landing and paddle out the way I came in the day before.

It is eerily still as I dip the shovel and paddle forward. Besides the small ripples coming off our boat as we cut through the water, there is no motion around us, not even a drip from the ceiling above.

"There!" Kota says, pointing forward. "I think that is the exit."

The opening ahead is only a few shades brighter than the rest of the area, but it is clearly the way out. I put my shovel back in the boat and move closer to the motor.

"Cross your fingers," I tell Kota, grabbing the handle of the pull cord. "If you see anything that seems dangerous, yell."

Kota clicks the light off, and I use all my might to rip the cord upward as hard as I can. The motor sputters for a moment and then kicks to life, propelling the boat quickly toward the circular exit. My heart rate is increasing the closer we get to the light, and I realize my hand is shaking even though my body is warm.

We both duck as the boat jets through the opening, and for our first time together, Kota and I are out of the garage and on top of the flooded earth.

"Do you see anything that might give you a clue where we are?" I yell above the roar of the motor. "Get out the map!"

Kota is perched at the front of the boat, scanning the water as we continue forward to nowhere. It doesn't feel like it's raining too hard now, but the mist is so thick, my jacket is already covered with accumulated droplets that are running down to my pants.

"Kota!" I yell again. "The map!"

"I'm going!" Kota yells back as he spins around and reaches immediately into the backpack. There is a panic and intensity in his voice. "Keep looking for Dark Pools!"

We emerge out of the mist and glide into a pocket of still weather. It seems like we are in the eye of a hurricane, because I can see layers of mist all around, but we aren't entering any of it. The area seems to be swallowed by an eerie, white shroud.

I am about to ask Kota about the map again when I notice something ahead. Small ripples are forming odd patterns, like invisible stones being tossed into the lake without a splash. The ripples begin to merge together and take the form of a circle.

I grip the edge of the boat with my left hand and squeeze my other on the handle of the motor to stop myself from shaking.

"Kota!" I scream. "Look!"

As if the water itself is being devoured, a large, gaping black circle quickly forms a few feet ahead of the boat. There is no depth to it, like someone suddenly placed a large, black disk flat on the surface of the water.

"Turn around!" Kota screams, his hands locked on both sides of the boat. "Go back to the parking garage!"

I yank the handle of the motor to the left, and the back of the boat swings hard around, sending a wave of water directly at the Dark Pool. The wave crashes over the void and vanishes into the black without making a sound.

I jam the handle in the other direction, which sends the boat skipping toward the other side of the Dark Pool. I only get a quick glimpse of it before Kota shouts again.

"Look out! Shui gui! Shui gui!"

Another Dark Pool is forming ahead of the bow. Kota slams himself into the side of the boat as I pull the handle back to the right. The boat does a heavy lean, and for a second, I think we are about to tip. But the blade of the motor continues to spin, and just before we topple into the water, the boat corrects itself and shoots us forward, just missing the outside of the second Dark Pool.

A plume of smoke shoots up from the motor, and I turn to avoid inhaling the chemicals. I see the two Dark Pools; they are leaving almost as quickly as they formed, dissipating into smaller ripples, and eventually disappearing completely.

I whip my head around to see if more are forming. The surrounding mist has left, the rain has slowed, and for the first time, I can see hundreds of feet in front of us.

Kota is now standing up holding the map, frantically looking around in all directions. I do the same, taking in the new view of trees just poking above the water as Kota yells.

"Look over there! See that?"

In the distance, just visible above the tree line and the tops of smaller buildings, is a metal dome standing about twenty to thirty feet above the water.

"That's a water tower! Head that way!" shouts Kota.

I turn the handle of the boat as my eyes continue to scan the water for another sign of a Dark Pool.

"The water tower sits over the Bucknell River. I know where we are! I've been here before! Don't stop!"

"Are you sure?!" I yell back, and straighten up as best I can while keeping one hand steady on the handle of the motor. I am paranoid that another Dark Pool will suddenly form, and Kota must be, too, because his head is on a swivel.

Ten seconds goes by.

Twenty seconds.

Thirty seconds.

"I'm gonna cut the motor for a second!" I yell. "We need to save the gas!"

I hit the red button and send the boat back into a quiet coast as I put the shovel in the water and paddle. The water tower is only a few hundred yards away.

"We just need to get a little closer so I can use the compass to be sure!" Kota shouts, eyes now fixed on the map. "But I think I can get us pointed in the right direction!"

Heavier rainfall begins the moment Kota finishes his sentence, changing from a light start to a straight downpour within just a few seconds. Kota and I scramble to get the tarp over us and the boat before taking on water.

Kota is completely focused now. He has the map spread out on the bottom of the boat, and the sleeve of his jacket is hovering above it as he alternates between viewing the compass and looking out from under the tarp to see our surroundings.

I'm on high alert as I do my best to look for any moment a Dark Pool could form again.

At first, I think I see another.

But as we get closer, I realize there are multiple small domes of earth poking up above the surface of the water. They still have some vegetation on them: sagging plants hanging over each other, small trees with most of their branches snapped in half, and grass that looks more like seaweed as the water rushes over the top.

Kota must see something I don't, though, because his excitement grows while my fear of the Dark Pools lingers.

"Oh! This is it!" he yells, pointing to a mound of mud about as wide as a school bus, just to the east of the water tower. He puts one finger on the map, then rotates it underneath his thumb until the map is facing the opposite direction.

"Did you figure it out?" I ask, pulling the tarp forward to better protect Kota and the map. "Which way do we go?"

"Definitely this way," Kota says, gesturing outside as he rechecks his compass. "We'll go around the water tower and keep heading this way, south." He turns his head around until he is facing me, like he is looking for approval.

"I trust you," I confirm, even though I don't really

have a choice at this point. I stick the shovel back in the water and paddle in the direction Kota pointed, just to the outside of the water tower. The rain is still streaking down the sky in large, powerful streams, but it is not penetrating through the tarp resting on our heads. We are dry, for now.

Kota sticks his head out the front and looks up to the side.

"Uh, Aurora?" he calls out. "What does *that* mean?"

I pull the shovel in and shuffle forward until I am at the bow of the boat with Kota. Even with the rain blanketing the sky, I can still make out what he is pointing to.

On the side of the metal domed water tower, spray-painted in giant red letters, is a warning:

STAND WITH THE HILL
OR DO NOT STAND AT ALL.

Chapter 15

Is that, um, a threat?" Kota asks. "Why would someone climb that high to write it? Did they mean to write 'stand *on* The Hill'? Or maybe . . ."

Kota continues to rattle off questions as fast as he can think of them, but I am not sure how to answer, especially the first one.

Is that a threat?

"I don't know anything about The Hill," I admit, tucking my head back beneath the protection of the tarp. "But this makes me think a lot of people know about it, a lot more than I thought."

"Is that a bad thing?" Kota questions, his face scrunching up.

"I don't think so?" I say half-heartedly. "I mean, we have a map, and The Hill seems to be a safe haven."

"Wait, what do you mean?" Kota presses. "I thought the map was yours."

He looks at me with his head cocked to the side, like a dog does when you ask a question it obviously doesn't understand. If Kota and I are going to trust each other to navigate the water together, then he deserves the truth. All of it.

"The map *is* mine, kind of," I admit. "You should probably know the whole story."

I stick the shovel back into the water and recap everything from the moment I arrived at Niko and Jada's mansion until the moment I met him in the parking garage.

Kota doesn't interrupt to ask anything, which is strange considering how much he asked after seeing the message on the water tower. But when I get to the end of my story, he has one question.

"So . . . what *is* The Hill, then?" he asks while sticking his hand out from underneath the tarp to check the rain. "Do you know *anything* about it?"

"I don't," I admit. "But I believe it's somewhere we can go to be safe. If Niko and Jada had plans to go there—and they *always* have a plan—then it must be safe for you and me too."

"If it's so safe," Kota snaps, "then why didn't they take you with them?"

His question cuts straight through the confidence I've been trying to feel since I left the mansion. But the truth is, Kota is right. I do not know where they are or why they disappeared. The thought of them being captured is haunting, and so is the idea of them crawling through the window and leaving me while I was fast asleep. It hurts in a way I can't quite explain, but I can't let Kota know that yet. Some things are meant to be kept to yourself, especially if you don't have an answer for them.

"I am not sure why they left, but I do believe this is the place they were planning to take us, so there must be a good reason," I say as Kota removes the tarp from his head. The rain is back to a drizzle now, which means I can paddle a bit faster. "The Hill is safe. It has to be."

"I hope we can find it," he says, fully removing the tarp from above him. "Because I don't want to be on this boat forever."

"Same here," I agree.

I stop paddling so Kota and I can fold the tarp up together. We place it on top of the metal bench I've been sitting on to make a temporary cushion, and as I begin to paddle again, Kota checks the map and compass.

"How far do you think we have to go?" I ask, scanning the water for any danger. "A few miles?"

"Way more than that," Kota says while pointing above the still water. "If we go in a straight line, it'll be shorter, but I think it's over twenty miles, at least."

"I trust you, Kota," I say again, dipping the shovel back into the water. "But I hope you are wrong."

We continue in silence for the next couple hours, but it seems longer. Every movement in the water makes Kota and me straighten, ready for another Dark Pool to form next to us. Kota's stories about them don't calm me down either.

"Grandma said the shui gui are here because they have unfinished business on earth."

"Why would they want to hurt anyone, then?" I counter, trying to distract myself from the fear that keeps bubbling up as I paddle. "Shouldn't they just go finish what they need to?"

Kota thinks for a second, then comes up with an answer he doesn't seem to like.

"Grandma said they come back to take people who need to be taken," he says, and then pauses, like a new realization is settling in. "But why did they take Grandma and Baba? They were good people."

Kota looks at me as if I have an answer. Even though I don't, I give him one anyway.

"I'm sure your grandma and dad didn't do anything wrong," I affirm. "I'm not sure if I believe in water ghosts, but if they do exist, then they made a mistake taking them."

Kota looks out over the water again, taking in the view and maybe my answer. He was right about one thing, at least—the Dark Pools *are* real—but what they actually are is still a mystery to me. I just hope we don't encounter one again.

As I scan the surface of the water with Kota, there is a lot more to take in as we head farther south, and none of it is encouraging. We must be passing through another neighborhood or town because the first thing we see is a school, or what used to be one.

It's strange how something so deeply submerged in water can still be recognizable. The first thing I see is a scoreboard that reads HOME OF THE PANTHERS, but the mascot's face is half submerged in the brown water. There is also a flagpole next to it, with a soggy fabric wrapped around the pole like it is trying to stay out of the water.

"I don't recognize the mascot or the school," Kota says, pointing to the scoreboard. "Do you?"

"Not at all," I say, looking around. "But I know it's not mine."

I can't believe I'm thinking this, but I miss school.

I never belonged anywhere, not really, but at least school was the one thing that didn't change when I was shuffled from one foster home to the next. No matter where I slept, no matter what house I had to learn the rules of, I still walked through the same front doors every morning, still sat in the same rows of desks, still saw the same faces in the halls.

I had a couple of friends. Not the kind you tell secrets to, not the kind who save you a seat at lunch or invite you over on weekends. But they were there. A presence. A constant. People I could laugh with in class, complain about assignments with.

I wonder where they are now. If they made it to high ground with their families. If they're safe. If they're scared. If they even had time to think about me before everything fell apart.

As we get closer to the school, the boat snags on

something for the first time, and I can see what it is: a basketball hoop.

The backboard of a basketball hoop, to be more specific. I take the shovel and wedge it between the backboard and the boat to pry us loose, then lay the shovel across the middle of the boat to steady us.

We are lucky we haven't hit anything else since we can't see what's beneath the water, and hitting the hoop makes me more mindful of how careful we must be as we navigate through the schoolyard, or what is left of it.

"I remember when school let out for the summer," Kota says, turning his entire body around to face me on the bench. "How long were we out before the rain started?"

"Only a week or so," I say as we glide pass the second floor of the school. "We didn't get much of a summer vacation, did we?"

"I was supposed to go on a weeklong Scouts trip," Kota mentions as he goes through the extra materials in the boat. "We were gonna go hiking, have late-night campfires, and . . . wait!"

Kota snatches the five-foot piece of rope we found earlier and holds it up for me to see. "And we were gonna go fishing! I think I can use this to fish!"

"The rope's too thick, isn't it?" I ask. "Won't the fish, like, see it or something?"

"Rope is just made up of tiny little strings," he explains as he separates the top part of the rope with his fingers. "We can just use one of those and attach it to the side of the boat instead of using a fishing pole!"

For the next few minutes, Kota separates the rope into a bunch of smaller threads. Part of me wants to keep the rope intact for something else, like tying off the boat if we need to, but since my stomach had been gurgling all morning, catching fish seems way more important.

"Okay, time to fish!" Kota declares, and digs into the backpack to reveal the fly hooks he made the day before.

I want to keep watching him work, but the school buildings are getting closer together, and we can't afford to crash into anything. So while Kota fastens the flies to the strings and the strings to the boat, I keep watch over the water.

The objects that float by are a constant reminder that people used to be here. A purple baseball hat brushes up against the boat, followed by a laundry basket a few moments later. Sometimes the debris is so thick and close together I can't see the water anymore, and it takes so much effort to push it aside that I barely have enough energy to resume paddling when we get through it.

If Kota is right—that we have at least twenty more miles to go—then we need food, or we are never going to make it.

"I need a break," I say, plopping the shovel across

my lap. "I'm going to try and lie down for a second. Can you paddle for a bit?"

Kota seems to like that idea, because he stands up so quickly that the boat rocks and almost launches the shovel into the water.

"Whoops, I'm sorry," he apologizes. "Yeah, I can paddle."

We switch places, and for the first time in hours, I lie flat on my back and shut my eyes. I am too nervous to try and sleep, but just the simple act of not paddling makes me feel like my energy is coming back, if only barely. My shoulders ache, and my hands feel stuck in the same grip they use to hold the makeshift paddle, not to mention that my head still throbs each time I breathe in and out. Still, listening to the rhythmic sound of the shovel entering and leaving the water is soothing, and my body is able to relax for a while as Kota sinks the paddle in and out of the water.

In . . . and out.

In . . . and . . . out.

In . . . and . . . out . . .

"Aurora? Aurora, wake up! We have a fish!"

I struggle to sit up as the boat pitches back and forth. Kota is at the left side of the vessel, both hands in the water.

“Oh my gosh, I actually caught one!” he yelps as he pulls the line out of the water. “Look at this guy!”

I am foggy. I didn’t even realize I had fallen asleep until the moment I heard Kota. I don’t know how long I’ve been out or where we are, but all my worry goes away when Kota pulls the fish fully out of the water.

I’ve never caught a fish, but this seems like a big one. It’s at least a foot long and has flickers of color shining off its scales.

Kota throws its flopping body into the boat. Before I can think of how to help before the fish bounces out, Kota picks it back up and smacks its head over the bench.

The sudden loss of life makes me cover my mouth.

“Oh, I’m sorry,” Kota says, removing the soda-can hook from the fish’s mouth. “I should have warned you first.”

I lower my hands and lean over Kota and the fish.

“It’s okay,” I assure him. “I’ve just never, um, watched anyone do that before.”

“I felt that way the first time I went fishing with Baba,” Kota says as he throws the hook and line back into the water. “I know this sounds weird, but . . . do you want to touch it? That helped me the first time.”

Kota extends the fish to me, and I take my fingers and glide them along its slick scales and bright colors. I’ve never touched a fish before that wasn’t already cooked, which makes me realize the very real situation we are in.

And also makes me realize something else.

We have no way to cook the fish.

"What do we do now?" I ask.

"Well, we can eat it raw," Kota suggests. "But it's risky. We could get sick."

We stare at the fish, because we both know how this is going to end.

Without talking, Kota points to the hatchet on my hip. I remove it from its sheath and hand it over. Kota then sinks the sharp end of the blade into the belly of the fish. When he does, I have to turn away because I can't stand the sight.

A few moments later, Kota taps me on the shoulder. He is holding a light pink strip of meat with the scales still attached to the other side.

I dangle the piece in front of me as Kota does the same with his. He doesn't have the same look I do as I contemplate the risks of actually eating it, but before I can talk it through with him, he sinks his teeth into the side of the fish.

I watch to gauge his reaction. He chews for a second before swallowing, and then he goes back for a second bite.

That is all the confirmation I need.

I lift the fish to my face and take a moderate bite. It is not hard and firm, like I expect it to be, but slightly warm and mushy. It doesn't have much of a taste, either, and the smell isn't pleasant at all. But it is food. And that is what I need right now.

Kota and I each finish our pieces, and this time I watch as Kota cuts off another chunk. Then another. Within just a couple minutes, we devour the entire fish, leaving only the skin, backbone, and head.

"You did it!" I announce to Kota once we're done. "You got us a fish!"

Kota has a goofy grin, and if it weren't for the cold rain picking back up and sticking to our faces, I would bet he is blushing too.

"Thanks," he says, lifting up another line from the side of the boat. "I'm going to put some of the skin on this hook and see if that attracts another one, for later."

"I'll tie us off somewhere for the night," I tell him. "It's getting dark, and the rain is increasing again."

Kota fastens the skin to the hook just as we pass a series of telephone poles. If it weren't for the giant, silver electrical cords that shoot out from them, they would look like remnants of an old boating dock. I use the shovel to guide us close and then grab the remainder of the rope to secure the boat tightly around one of the poles.

Together, Kota and I unfold the tarp and cover ourselves in the boat for the night. We lie right next to each other and pull the two blankets up to our chins, just like the giraffe and elephant back in the van. I expect it will take a while before either of us falls asleep, but it's not long before I hear Kota breathing deeply through his nose, his mouth hanging open.

I shift slightly, careful not to wake him.

We barely know each other, but I feel something growing in me as I watch him sleep. It's a type of pull I haven't felt before, or maybe one I've forgotten over the years. Even though we aren't family, lying here in the dark with him beside me, with our blankets pulled up to our chins, he feels like something just as important, and that is enough to comfort me.

At least for now.

Chapter 16

The sound of rain pelts the tarp all night long, and sleep comes in waves like the ones hitting the boat. Besides that, I must also contend with Kota, who thrashes in his sleep. I wake him up a couple times to get him to stop, and he does the same for me when I scream.

I didn't even know I was doing it.

By the morning, we are both exhausted, but at least the rain has backed off to a mist again, and the wind is now more of a gentle breeze. Plus, we are greeted with a delightful but disgusting surprise: Another fish is on the hook, but it doesn't look like the first.

"What is *that*?" I ask when Kota pulls the strange-looking creature into the boat.

"It's a type of catfish, I think," he says, removing the hook. "Look out, I have to . . ."

I turn around just at Kota clunks the fish's head onto the bench. He doesn't offer me the chance to touch it this time, and I don't want to. The whiskers coming out of the fish's head make it look more like an alien, and I don't want to look at it longer than I have to, especially because I know I have to eat it.

"I'll let you prep the fish while I untie the boat," I suggest as I untether us from the telephone pole. "Let's get moving as soon as possible."

The mist is so light that I remove my hood for the first time since leaving the parking garage, and Kota follows my lead. I look up at the sky, and instead of dark clouds that look like they are about to dump millions of gallons of water, they are orange and brown as the light from the sun attempts to penetrate their cover. But like every day since the rain came, the sun never pokes through.

Ever.

"Wow," Kota blurts out. "Take a look at that!"

Far ahead, I can see it again. It's the city skyline, and it's more visible than before. With the brown-and-orange clouds behind it, the city looks like a half-forgotten dream, shimmering just above the water. The tips of the tallest buildings poke out like a series of lighthouses, and in my mind I can hear the sounds of a bustling city, with thousands of people on their way to jobs and school and life.

But I also hear Niko's words, too, and they resonate louder than my imagination.

"The city is a death trap. A concrete, flooded death trap."

"I bet there are people there who can help us!" Kota announces excitedly. "And look, we have to pass right through it to get to The Hill!"

Kota lays the map out in front of him.

"We can't go there," I state firmly. "It's dangerous."

"Says who?" Kota argues as the boat sways. "We don't know anything about it."

"Exactly," I counter. "Which means it could be a disaster waiting to happen."

"Well . . ." Kota pauses. "We don't have a choice anyway. We can't go around it."

"Yes, we can," I argue, my voice growing louder. "Look around us! I don't see a barrier forcing us to go straight through the city, do you?"

"You want to add extra time by going *around* the city? You want to sleep another night out here?!" Kota asks, rising. "Because I don't! I want to get off the boat! I want to go to the—"

Without warning, the boat begins to tip backward, as if we are going down a hill. It is so sudden that Kota, who had been standing, loses his balance and falls forward onto the hull of the boat, which brings the back end even with the water's surface again. As I turn around to see what is causing the chaos, I see just enough black sitting on the water to know what it is—a Dark Pool.

I grab the shovel and thrust it into the water, pulling it back as hard as I can. The boat surges forward with the stroke, and I rip the shovel out again and plunge it back in for another.

I can barely hold on as I dig it into the water, my hands shaking with panic. My breaths come in short, frantic bursts, and I feel the boat wobble beneath us with each frantic stroke, like it wants to go under as the cold water splashes up into my face.

I snap my head around to see how far I've managed to get us away from danger. It isn't much, but the Dark Pool doesn't seem to be expanding any further and instead holds still, like a black hole in space. When I look back at Kota, I notice more of them ahead: dark, perfectly round circles, shifting on the surface like shadows, growing steadily as they merge into one another.

I drop the shovel and finally yank the cord of the motor. It sputters, then dies.

"The shui gui are back!" I hear Kota yell from the front. "There's too many of them!"

I give the cord another pull, and the motor turns over, shooting a stream of water up from behind the boat as we lurch forward. The burst of speed lifts the tarp off the bottom of the boat and sends it past my face before I can attempt to grab it. The map lifts up from the floor, too, while the wind swoops into the boat's interior.

"The map!" I holler. "Grab the map!"

Kota turns around and falls onto the floor, covering the map, and the catfish slides off the bench, bouncing around as the boat rips over the bumps of the choppy water. The Dark Pools are still forming, but we seem to be outpacing them as the patches become fewer and fewer. I keep my hand on the motor and steady it toward the one place that can get us out of this scenario.

The city.

The boat slams with each thing we bump into: wood, barrels, and other objects I can't identify because we are going faster than I have ever gone in the boat. The motor is making a high-pitched whistle that seems to be indicating its end, though I have no idea what it actually means—it just doesn't sound good.

"Are they gone?! The shui gui?" Kota yells over the squeal of the motor. "Can you see them?!"

I turn around to see a series of more Dark Pools. They seem to rise from nowhere, like whispers from another world. Each one follows the same pattern—forming, floating, shrinking—but somehow each one seems different.

"They are still there!" I yell back. "We need to keep going!"

Kota sits up and looks behind me to confirm, and then we both turn to look forward. It seemed far away a minute ago, but the city is now in full view as we charge through the water. The windows are becoming clearer, and more structures I couldn't make out before are now recognizable: lifted roads overlapping each other, interstate signs on bridges, and highway lampposts moving past us. I don't give anything a second thought until I see a road coming up out of the water.

It continues toward the city, lifting high above the water on parallel concrete pillars. Cars and trucks are lined up against the guardrails, stretching as far as I can see, before the road curls into the center of the city skyscrapers and disappears.

We need to get out of the water now! We have to!

"Kota!" I call out above the high-pitched sound of the motor. "Get ready to jump out and grab hold of the boat! I'm gonna dock it up on that road!"

He grabs both sides and braces for impact as I cut the engine. We glide a few feet forward until I can feel the vibration of the road scraping the bottom of the boat. We come to a stiff halt, and Kota jumps out into the shallow edge of the water and latches on to the boat to prevent it from moving.

I scurry to the front, grab my hatchet, the map, and my backpack, and get out beside him. Together, the two of us drag the boat all the way out of the water into the middle of the ascending roadway.

We sit down to catch our breath as I look out to see where we came from. It's a chaotic waterscape of mass destruction. Homes that once stood tall are almost completely gone, some cars float like kids' toys in a filthy tub, and Dark Pools grow and shrink like the pupils of an eye.

What are those things?!

When I look over at Kota, I see he is laughing. I don't know if he's delirious or in shock, but his giggle makes me laugh as well, and soon the two of us embrace.

We made it out of the water. We actually made it.

"Can't say I've seen two kids make it this far on their own," a voice from behind us says.

Kota and I let go of each other and spin around to see three people emerge from behind a series of cars at the top of the sloped road. One of them, a woman, is dressed in all camouflage like a solider and holds a bat with something sharp sticking out of the top. The other two are men. One of them has a giant scar that runs across the entire length of his face, and the other is standing with his hands at his sides, like he's ready to grab something.

The woman takes a few more steps toward the edge of the road and angles her weaponized bat in our direction.

"Why don't you come up here?" she hollers from above. "And while you're at it, bring that boat of yours with you."

Chapter 17

I said, *bring that boat of yours with you!*" the woman yells again, with increasing agitation in her voice. "That, or you can go for a swim. Either way, we're taking the boat."

I look at Kota, who is staring at me like I have a solution, but I don't. Instead, I put my hands on the front of the boat, and Kota follows my lead as we attempt to lift the boat up the steep, bumpy slope of the road.

We don't get very far before the boat slams back to the ground.

"They can't do it," the man with the scar declares. "The boat's too heavy, and they're just kids."

"Well, then, you better go help them," the woman barks, pointing the bat in our direction again. "Hurry up, before someone sees us. We are vulnerable to an attack out here."

The man runs down the slope toward us and grabs the boat by its side, quickly flipping it upside down and hoisting it into the air like it weighs nothing. Our blankets and rope immediately fall to the ground, but he doesn't even notice them as he places the boat on his shoulders and makes his way back to the top of the road.

"Wait, what about us?" I plead as I pull the other strap of my backpack over my shoulder. "We need the boat!"

"Not as much as we do," the woman declares, tapping the wired bat on the ground. "But don't worry. You're coming with us until I can figure out what to do with you."

The other man comes down the slope and grabs Kota and me by the wrists. He gives us both a long, hard glare as his dirty, wet face scrunches into a ball to deliver a warning.

"Don't try anything stupid," he mutters. "Got it?"

Kota and I both nod as the man turns and yanks us toward the woman with the bat. Despite her strong voice, she looks weaker the closer we get. Her eyes are sunken into her head, and her hair is tangled and knotted. Even so, the sharp bat in her hand makes her seem much more powerful.

She turns and leads our group up the road, toward the heart of the city. No one is speaking, but both the woman and the man pulling us are keeping watch. Their heads are darting back and forth between the cars, like they are anticipating a visitor.

"Ow!" Kota yelps. "You're hurting my wrist!"

"Quiet!" the woman snaps. "You're gonna attract—"

Before she can finish, a figure lunges out from behind a car, wrapping their arms around her waist and slamming her into the pavement. Her bat slips from her grasp, bouncing and clanging as it skids down the road. Two more figures rush out from behind another car, pinning her hands to the ground before she can fight back.

BANG!

I whip my head around just in time to see the boat crash to the ground. Another pair of attackers emerges, assaulting the man with the boat and striking him hard across the face before he can react.

It's an ambush.

A sharp scream pulls my attention to my side. I turn to see Kota sinking his teeth into the hand of the man gripping us. The attacker snarls in pain, grabs a fistful of Kota's hair, and throws him to the ground. Before he can do more, another man charges in and tackles him, sending them both sprawling.

I dart forward, grabbing Kota and pulling him to his feet.

"Run!" I yell, and we bolt forward toward the city without looking back. The shouts and screams behind us are all the motivation I need to keep running. My heart pounds as we weave through the chaos.

"Run *faster!*" I holler at Kota, who keeps looking backward. "We need to hide!"

I take Kota by the hand as the elevated road bends toward the inner city, our first chance for safety.

"Over there!" I yell.

Past the edge of the raised road and across a few feet of water is an emergency exit ladder clinging to the side of a crooked brick building. But the closer we get, the more damage I see. The corroded brackets are barely holding the ladder in place, and the building itself is equally deteriorating, with cracked and discolored bricks outlining the shattered windows.

"We can make it!" I shout as we close the gap to the ladder, now within jumping distance.

"I can't!" Kota yells back, panic in his voice. "I'll fall in the water!"

I glance over my shoulder and spot the attacking group turning toward us, their fingers already pointing in our direction. I whip back around to face the building, plant both feet firmly on the ground, and push off with a desperate leap. My body slams into the ladder; I clutch the cold, rusted rungs tightly to steady myself.

"They're coming!" Kota cries. "Help me!"

I scramble a few rungs higher and stretch out my hand. As soon as his fingers clasp mine, I pull with every ounce of strength I have. His feet skim the surface of the water before he crashes into the ladder and snags it with trembling hands.

Then I get up as quickly as I can. The rusted metal groans under my weight with each step. When I reach the first shattered window, I pause. Jagged shards of glass are sticking out of the frame, sharp enough to tear through my clothes, or worse, my skin. I pull out my hatchet and knock the shards loose, sending them clinking to the floor inside. Once the way is clear, I climb through, gripping the unstable ladder frame for balance.

Inside, the floor, like the building, is sloped dramatically, and I struggle to stand as I turn to help Kota through. I grab his arm and drag him over the windowsill. The floor threatens to throw me off balance.

"We need to keep going!" I shout. Kota attempts to stand and catch his breath. "We need to hide!"

We frantically stumble our way through the dilapidated apartment. The furniture has all slid down to one side against the farthest wall, making it seem like we are on a sinking ship instead of in a building. The entry door ahead is open, and we brace ourselves against its frame as we enter the hallway.

"Over there!" Kota says. "Stairs!"

He is right, but they do not resemble stairs as much as they do a collection of broken wooden planks, which don't even reach the next floor. Instead, they go halfway up, revealing an open gap to the floor above.

The tinging sound of metal on metal alerts both of us as we look back to the window we came in. The supports of the ladder are shifting.

Someone must be coming up!

"Go! Go! Go!" I holler, directing Kota toward the steps. He pushes off the frame of the door and awkwardly runs toward the stairs, tripping a few times as he struggles to maintain his balance. I follow closely until we reach the stairwell, where Kota wastes no time climbing it.

The top floorboard buckles under his weight. I lunge, grabbing his ankle as it plunges into the rotted wood. I heave his foot back as he grasps for the solid edge of the floor above.

"Hurry, Kota!" I beckon.

Kota pulls himself up, his chest sprawled on the overhang as his arms strain for leverage. I don't wait. Gripping the rail, I start after him, but the stairs are treacherously slick and unsteady, shifting beneath me like stacks of ice blocks.

"Take my hand!" Kota yells from above. He's flat on his stomach now, with one arm outstretched toward me.

I lunge upward, clasping his hand just as the shattering crash of glass echoes from somewhere down the hallway. Kota pulls with everything he's got, relieving the pressure from my slipping feet. With his help, I claw my way up, finally collapsing beside him on the upper floor.

"Where'd they go?!" a deep voice bellows in the distance. "They can't be far!"

I tap Kota on the shoulder and put my finger over my mouth.

"Crawl," I hoarsely whisper.

Then we slowly creep our way down the crooked

hallway to the first open door on the right as the voices continue.

"What about the stairs?!" the voice yells.

"Just look at 'em!" another answers. "Ain't no way anyone getting up those steps."

The voices continue while Kota and I enter the room, which looks similar to the first one we entered. All the furniture has slid to the side: an upside-down couch, a broken television, and a toppled leather chair. I point to an opening between the couch and the wall it is leaning against, and together we crawl into the cushioned cave while we listen.

"It's not worth it," announces the voice from below, the sound of shifting wood planks punctuating his sentence. "They could be anywhere, and we need to get the boat back to camp before someone else sees what we got."

I look at Kota, whose face I can barely see in the darkness of our fort. I hold my finger in front of my mouth again, and we both stay still. Seconds turn into minutes, and the minutes stretch into a time that feels longer than it probably is.

"I need to . . . go to the bathroom," Kota whispers, breaking the long stretch of silence. "Do you think it's safe to stand up?"

I shift my body so I can stick my head out the opening and around the corner of the couch. I can't hear anything except the rain outside. It seems safe to move.

"Okay, we can get out," I whisper. "But we need to stay quiet."

Kota squeezes past me before I can get to my feet and heads toward an opening to the next room. I can hear the familiar sound of a toilet lid hitting the tank, so I assume he has found the bathroom.

For the first time since leaving the mansion, I'm surrounded by walls. Real walls. Not the endless stretch of sky above the boat; not the cold, open air of the parking garage. The ceiling here sags, and the walls are cracked and stained, but they stand. The air is thick with dust and something stale, but at least it is dry, not like the humidity of the storm pressing down outside.

It's not much, but it feels like a luxury.

I let myself breathe it in, just for a second.

As I pause, I notice things in the dim light that I didn't when we first entered. There is a family picture dangling by a wire on the far wall: two parents and four kids, all posing in front of a cabin. Next to that picture is another, this time the four kids in front of a large body of water—maybe the ocean? There are more pictures on the wall, too, and each one is full of ear-to-ear family smiles.

Must be nice to be happy all the time.

I've never even been on a family vacation.

I continue browsing the images of the picture-perfect family, but something catches my eye because it's out of place. Slightly overlapping two of the photos, nailed between them, is a single sheet of lined paper.

I take a few steps forward and realize what it is.

A letter.

I click my flashlight on to get a better view and scan the handwritten note.

> Jeanene,
>
> I've tried calling you countless times, every day until the power went out. I have enough food to last a few more days, but I can't wait any longer. I can only hope you and the kids are safe, wherever you are.
>
> If you find this letter, it means I've left the city. A neighbor heard mention of a safe place called The Hill, and I am going to try to reach it, though I'm not even sure where it is. I'm planning to check the canoe in the storage area, if I can even access it.
>
> I love you all so much. I pray every day I'll find you.
>
> —Markell

I reread the letter, hoping I missed something that might be helpful, as questions swarm inside my head.

This Markell. He knows about The Hill?!

How many people know about it?

How come I didn't know about it?!

Why didn't Niko and Jada tell me about it?

I take a few steps back, and the pictures of the family come back into view. A happy family, with plenty of pictures to prove it, torn apart by the state of the world.

How many other families are searching for each other?

Is anyone searching for me? Are Niko and Jada?

I abruptly turn away from the wall and click my flashlight off because I know the answer.

No one is looking for me.

But I wish someone was.

A flicker of daylight to the right catches my eye, by an opening to another room. I take one last glance at the letter before taking tiny steps toward the light, trying to avoid falling on the slanted floor and creating a loud noise that could alert the attackers.

I slowly creep along until I find myself in a small kitchen. The blue-tinted cabinets are all open, their contents spilled onto the floor. There are pots, pans, and broken bowls, but there are also some cans. Food, maybe.

Before I can investigate further, Kota joins me in the kitchen.

"You're hurt!" Kota points out. "Your arm!"

I look down at my exposed forearm, which has nothing but my birthmark.

"It's all right," I assure him, pulling my sleeve over the three markings. "It's just a birthmark. Are you okay?"

"I think so," he says, staring at my now-covered

arm. "Why did those people attack the others? Why didn't they help us?"

"Niko told me the city wasn't safe," I say, reflecting on the conversation. "He said people would turn on each other, and I guess he was right."

"But we didn't even *do* anything," Kota responds, clearly still stuck on the thought. "Shouldn't everyone be helping . . . well, everyone?"

"Yeah, you'd think," I say. "Especially two kids."

Kota shakes his head as I shuffle past him to the kitchen window, which has a small curtain loosely covering it. I use a single finger to pull back one side and get my first good glimpse of the city.

After the journey we just went through, it's surprising to see how quiet it is. There must have been thousands and thousands of people here before the rain came, so where are they now? Are they holed up, locked away in their apartments waiting for the rain to stop? Did they flee? Where are the helpers? The firefighters? The guards?

Where are all the people?

Jada had the same thought, about two weeks after the rain started, when it was clear the entire globe was facing the same situation.

"I'm sure the government has deployed the army by now, or at least local first responders," she said one morning, as we scraped the mold off the baseboards of the hallway. "I'm sure there is a system in place for this sort of thing."

"The ratios don't add up," Niko said. "Think about how many people are in the world compared to how many of them are first responders. There aren't enough people to help other people."

"Well, surely each city can coordinate some sort of relief," she said, dumping more rotten pieces of wood into the bucket. "The world can't go on without a plan."

"The world doesn't have a plan," Niko quipped. He pointed his scraper at Jada. "Because the world we know has stopped. And when the world stops, people will do what they have always done: Find their own way forward first."

Their own way forward.

TAP, TAP, TAP.

Kota's tapping on the window brings me back as we both stare into the flooded streets of the city. There are no helpers in sight. The only thing is the rushing of the water between the leaning buildings.

"So, what do we do now?" Kota asks, tapping the window again. "What's the plan?"

"I'm not sure," I admit. "But I think we are trapped."

Chapter 18

A new fear takes over as I stare out the window.

In the boat, we had a plan. Even though it was complicated, knowing we were heading somewhere was enough to keep me focused and motivated to push through the hunger and the pain of rowing the boat. I was scared, but not in a way that deterred me from trying.

But here, in the city that Niko warned about? I am *terrified.* I'm trapped inside of it, and I have no idea what to do next.

"Maybe we could try and find someone who can help us?" Kota offers as he joins me at the window. "There must be someone here who can help."

I close the curtains and lean against the sloped countertop.

"We don't know who is friendly and who isn't," I state matter-of-factly. "Just look at what happened to us! What if all the groups are like the attackers on the road?"

Kota doesn't respond. Instead, he crouches and

rifles through the scattered cans on the floor. He picks one up and turns it slowly in his hands until the label is fully visible, revealing an image of a pie. His eyes narrow as he reads.

"Easy . . . Pumpkin . . . Pie . . . Mix," he says. "Is this something we can eat?"

"I'm not sure," I admit as I join him on the floor. "Let's keep looking."

There isn't a ton of light in the apartment with the curtains drawn, so I take the flashlight out of my pocket to illuminate the other cans.

"Whoa, this person must have really liked pie," Kota points out as the light reflects off the orange of the other cans. "I don't see anything else."

"That's a shame," I mutter, crouching to grab another can of pie filling. I turn it over in my hands, scanning the ingredients with a frown. "I honestly have no idea what this stuff is."

"Well . . . can we eat it?" Kota asks again.

"We can try, I guess," I say while my own stomach calls out at the thought of food. "But we need a can opener."

As Kota and I stand back up and go through drawers, I realize this is the only plan we should have right now: finding food. We can't try to do anything unless we know where food is coming from.

"Got one!" Kota declares, pulling a can opener from the back of an open drawer. He snatches up a can of pie mix from the floor and starts cranking it open.

I've never been as interested in the contents of a single can as I am right now.

Kota peels back the lid, revealing an orangey-brown paste. He tilts the can toward his hand, expecting the filling to slide out, but it doesn't budge—it's too thick, clinging stubbornly to the sides.

Kota doesn't seem fazed.

With a casual shrug, he plunges his index finger into the center of the paste, scooping out a hefty glob. Without hesitation, he shoves it into his mouth, chewing with a look that's equal parts curiosity and determination. Before he even swallows, his finger goes back in the can for another scoop.

I take the can opener, remove the top of another can, and take my first bite of pumpkin pie mix. My tongue is met with a soft, cold texture I can only describe as old peanut butter, and the taste is bland, like I'm eating a vegetable that desperately wants to be something sweeter. Niko would've hated it too, just like he did the rations Jada had bought.

"I'm not eating this again until it's the *last* thing we have," Niko said once as he gulped down a mixture of mushy peas for dinner during the third week of rain. "Why on earth did you buy this stuff, Jada?"

"*PrepHer Magazine* said that vegetables and greens will be the hardest resources to come by if there is a natural disaster, so I bought as much as I could," she replied. "I don't think it's *that* bad. What do you think, Aurora?"

"It's not my favorite," I admitted, pushing my spoon to form a small cave within the peas, which had more of a mashed-potato texture. "It's better than nothing, though."

"Maybe so, but now I need something else to get this nasty taste out of my mouth," Niko declared, and stood up. "Jada, I think we should do it now."

"I figured you couldn't wait any longer," she shrugged, as she brought another spoonful to her mouth. "All right. Let's do it now."

"Do what now?" I piped up. But Niko didn't respond. Instead, he disappeared for just a moment and then returned, standing at the end of the makeshift kitchen table.

"We know it's not for a few more days," Niko started, "and I wish it was during better circumstances, but this is for you." He brought his hands forward, revealing a plate of chocolate cupcakes, each one with a little candle at the top, lined up to make the number seventeen.

"Happy birthday!" he said. "Hope you like chocolate. Had to run the genny all night to get the stove hot enough to make 'em. But hey, thankfully Jada here got some cupcake mix when she could."

"Happy birthday, Aurora!" Jada chimed in.

I stared down at the plate, taking in the sweet smell of the sugary frosting beneath the flicker of the candles. And even though chocolate wasn't my favorite, my smile would've made you think otherwise.

"I'd sing," Niko continued, "but you don't want to hear that. Trust me."

"Well, then, I'll do it," Jada announced.

While she sang, with Niko chiming in off-key, I thought about the other birthdays I'd had at the foster center. There was always cake. Sometimes ice cream. Candles, if someone remembered. And always the same wish.

But as I blew out the candles in front of Niko and Jada, I didn't wish for something that was missing. Because for once, it felt like maybe, just maybe, even in the rain, all those wishes could finally come true.

I try to think of the moist, gooey center of those cupcakes as Kota and I continue to push the paste into our mouths, but it doesn't really help mask the taste of the pie mixture. Within a few minutes, though, Kota has finished the entire can and starts to open another.

"Wait," I say as I put my hand gently on top of his. "We need to save this."

"But I'm hungry." Kota looks longingly at the can.

"Me too," I agree, "but we need to see how much food we actually have and think about how long it will last us."

I shine my light across the kitchen floor, counting silently in my head, which Kota must be doing as well.

"I only see eight," he says, looking back at me.

"That's what I got too," I concur, and then make a suggestion. "How about we plan on four cans each day? Two for me, two for you. That gives us two days of food."

"Deal," Kota says, and begins opening up the second can.

I don't think he cares how much we get each day as long as he gets to eat another can immediately. I eat mine slower, trying to process what our next steps could be, when Kota pauses to speak up.

"We should sleep here tonight," he suggests, then circles his finger in the can to get all remaining globs of the mix. "We could block the door, too, just in case."

I don't want to stay here, but I also don't know where else we would go.

"Okay, we can stay," I agree. "I just hope that's the right choice."

After finishing our pumpkin pie mix, we push the couch across the room until it is up against the front door, making it difficult for anyone to enter in the middle of the night. Then we head to the only room we haven't been in yet: the bedroom.

There's not much there.

The bed sits in the corner, its sheets still tucked neatly beneath the mattress, as if it's been frozen in time. The dresser, on the other hand, is tipped over, its drawers splayed open in a messy scene. Next to it is an open suitcase resting awkwardly against the bed frame with clothes spilling out, like someone left in the middle of packing it.

Kota steps over the mess and slips under the thick

comforter of the bed without a word. For the first time since we left the boat, I shrug off my backpack, letting it dangle by one strap from the bedpost. I slide in beside Kota, the heavy warmth of the covers enveloping us. Neither of us speaks as the last traces of daylight fade from the room.

If I dreamed at all, I don't remember it, likely because I spent most of the night awake, or at least it felt that way. Unfamiliar noises startled me, and every time I heard something, I was convinced someone was in the apartment with us, including when Kota gets out of bed in the morning.

"It's just me," Kota reassures as my head jolts up from the pillow and back down again. "I'm getting some pie mix. Do you want some?"

"Not yet," I say, rubbing my eyes.

Kota slips into the kitchen, leaving me alone as the heavy fog of exhaustion lifts from my body. I want to move, to tackle our problem head-on, but my mind and body refuse to align. My body knows that waking up means coming back to the reality of our situation, and it doesn't want to deal with it. I know we need to leave, to search for more food, but the physical fear has me frozen in place.

What happens if people find us? What if they aren't friendly? What will they do to us?

Kota returns, already halfway through his first can of the day, and he is eager for a plan.

"I was thinking we could just sleep here a few days and see what happens," he suggests, licking the pumpkin paste from his fingers. "No one will find us if we just stay in this place."

"I agree we are safer in here," I admit, and shift to a sitting position. "But I also don't want to stay until we run out of food. We need to get ahead of the problem."

"So what should we do?" Kota asks.

"I really don't want to," I say as I move out from under the covers while checking the wound on the back of my head. "But at some point, we need to leave and go find more food."

Kota nods, then pauses for a second.

"Wait, do you hear that?" he says, his head turning toward the door. "Is that . . . people?"

I quickly get up and walk over to the kitchen window, and my body searches for energy to meet the moment. Gently, I pull the curtain aside, my fingers trembling as I peer out. The noise's source comes quickly into focus—it's a rowdy crowd gathering on the raised road below, where Kota and I landed the boat yesterday. The longer I look, the larger the crowd becomes as people join from all sides of the road. Some are floating just beyond the road on what appear to be just planks of wood tied together, while others come directly out of parked vans on the raised street. It's like the whole city is waking up at the same time.

But there is no morning grogginess here. It's a commotion. And although I can't tell what they're saying, I can hear the anger in their voices.

"What is it?" Kota asks, and moves beside me.

My chest tightens as I watch the tension build in the group. There's people pointing at each other, people yelling, and people pumping their fists into the air. Suddenly, one person shoves another, and the group erupts into a frenzied brawl with fists flailing and shouts slicing through the air.

"The city is a death trap. A concrete, flooded death trap . . ."

I close the curtain and glance at Kota, who is covering his mouth.

"It's okay," I say, resting a hand on his shoulder. "They don't know we're here, and we'll keep it that way. Let's go."

Kota moves past me and rips the curtain open again.

"Why are they doing that to each other?!" he blurts out, putting both hands on the window. "Why are they fighting?!"

Kota looks at me as if I have an answer. I wish I did. I wish I could tell him something that would calm him down and make him realize everything is going to be okay.

I also wish I had someone to tell me the exact same thing.

I step forward to the window and peer down at the fighting below. Some of the crowd has gotten back on their rafts, but others are continuing to fight, their shouting growing even louder.

"We're safe here," I say, surprised at the words coming out of my own mouth. "We just need to be careful."

I place my hands on Kota's shoulders, and without looking back, he puts his hand on top of mine.

"You'll protect me?" he asks, still watching the fighting below.

I can feel Kota's words resonate through my entire body. I know what he is feeling because I have felt it for years. That longing for protection, for comfort, for stability.

"Yes," I state, as confidently as I can. "I will."

I'm locked in now, completely focused. Something about standing here with Kota is bringing me a new energy. Fear still simmers beneath the surface, but the determination I feel growing in me sharpens my core.

I will do this.

I will protect Kota.

I will get us where we need to go.

We will make it.

We will.

I walk back to the bedroom and sling the backpack over my shoulder, my fingers brushing the handle of the hatchet as I unclip it from my hip.

"Wait," Kota says, his voice hesitant. "Are we going somewhere?"

"We are," I say with certainty. "We're going to find food."

Chapter 19

"But what about all those people below?" Kota asks, almost yelling. "If we get caught out there, we're dead!"

"Shhh! Quiet!" I reprimand Kota. "You keep yelling like that and we *will* get caught."

"It's too dangerous," he whimpers. "We don't even know where to go or what kind of people are out there!"

I use one hand to guide Kota away from the window until he is facing me, and I stoop to get to eye level.

"We aren't leaving the building." I smile. "In fact, we'll just check the apartments on this floor and the floor above. Then we'll come back."

"And eat?" Kota asks.

"If we find more food, yes," I say, turning to look at the kitchen. "Come on, follow me."

I guide Kota over to the kitchen and rummage through the pile of objects on the floor until I find what I am looking for.

"I saw this yesterday and want you to carry it."

"Why?" Kota asks, taking the hammer from my hand. "Are we fixing something?"

"It's for protection," I say, tapping my hatchet. "I'd rather you carry a knife, but you might cut yourself carrying it around."

Kota stares at the hammer before tucking it into his belt loop. He stands a little taller as he takes a few practice steps to see how it feels.

"You look ready," I encourage. "Just like me."

"Yeah, just like you." Kota grins while looking at his hammer. "Okay, let's do it."

The two of us walk to the living room and move the couch away from the door and back up against the wall. The screeching of the wooden couch legs reminds me that we need to try our best to be silent, so I slowly turn the doorknob to try and avoid the inevitable click, but it doesn't work.

I pause for a moment to see if anything reacts to the sound.

Nothing. I think we can move.

I pull the door open and take a look down the hallway in each direction. There are many other apartment doors and a single, large window at one end of the hallway. Thunder claps, and a flash of lighting illuminates the space for just a moment before everything returns to its monotone appearance. It was short, but it gave me enough of a view to decide to head across the hall to the first open door.

I clasp my hatchet with one hand, ready to defend myself if I must. Before I enter the room, though, I glance back at Kota, who is mimicking me with his hand on the hammer.

"Ready?" I whisper.

Kota's eyes narrow, and he nods.

I slowly peek my head around the frame of the open door, and it's immediately clear that this apartment has also been abandoned, maybe even looted. The hanging television is smashed, with a piece of wood splintering out of a hole in the middle of the screen. Papers and envelopes are scattered everywhere, and all the furniture is knocked over.

"I'll check the kitchen," I inform Kota. "You go in the bedroom and see if there's anything we can use."

I move past the broken television as screams echo through the apartment from the flooded streets below. I choose not to look out the window. Instead, I open all the cabinets.

Nothing? Not a single box or can of food?

"I found something!" Kota announces too loudly from another room.

I head back to the living room, where Kota is holding a blue flashlight and an unopened pack of batteries.

"Looks like you have a flashlight now too," I say. "I'll put the batteries in my bag, but you hold on to that flashlight."

Kota grins and tucks the flashlight into his jacket

pocket before handing me the batteries. It's weird seeing something new, like it was just bought from the store. I can't even remember the last time I saw something in new packaging.

"Let's go to the next apartment," I suggest as I zip the backpack shut. "Your choice on which door."

"Cool." Kota gives me a thumbs-up. "But you lead the way."

We go back into the hallway, and Kota points to another open door, this one to the right of the elevator. Even though it's light enough to see inside, Kota clicks on his flashlight.

And just like the last one, this apartment is also destroyed.

Kota and I spend the next several hours going room to room in multiple apartments on our floor. Much of what we find doesn't dramatically change our situation: a few unopened water bottles, a candle, a box of matches with only five matchsticks, and a toy car I saw Kota sneak into his pocket, as if he might get caught taking it.

"I was really hoping we'd find food," Kota says, holding his stomach. "I don't think my body can handle any more pie mix today."

"Well, let's see if we can get to the next floor," I propose. "We have to at least try."

We ease back through the door and into the hallway again as the thunder rumbles and lightning flashes outside. Though the sounds of fighting have faded, I know that doesn't mean it's over. It makes me wonder what's happening in the deeper parts of the city, where we can't see or hear anything. In just one day, we've already witnessed multiple attacks.

Maybe Niko was right—maybe there really isn't anyone good left in the city.

As we continue down the hall, it becomes clear that the stairs to the next floor are not an option. There are only a few planks left clinging to the wall, and the rest of the wood and carpet sits in a giant heap. However, there is still a visible way up.

"There," I say, pointing to the seemingly random dresser next to the steps. "I think we can use that."

"Why would someone keep a dresser in the hallway?" Kota asks as he scans it with his flashlight. "That's strange."

"My guess is it was used as a step stool to get upstairs," I suggest, shaking the dresser to test its stability. "Want to go first?"

Kota shakes his head, so I put my hands on top and hoist my body up high enough to get a single knee on top of the dresser. Once I'm in a squat, I rise up and cautiously peek through the broken floor and into the hallway above.

"What do you see?" Kota asks from below.

"Nothing, really," I say. "Just another hallway."

I offer Kota my hand and pull him up onto the dresser. Kota steadies himself while I put my hands on the floor above, squeezing my body past the broken wood until I am fully in the new hallway. Kota does the same on his own, and he notices the first open door.

"Race you to the next one!" Kota shouts, running to the door ahead.

"What are you doing?!" I try not to yell, shocked by Kota's sudden change of attitude and energy. "Don't go in there yet! We have to move carefully!"

But by the time the last word comes out of my mouth, Kota is already inside the apartment.

"Kota, come back!" I say firmly.

Nobody responds.

"Kota, come on. This isn't funny."

Silence.

I can only assume he can't hear me because of the intermittent thunder, which is becoming even more frequent. Still, I throw my hands in the air in disgust, lecturing as I make my way to the door.

"We can't just run around yelling everywhere, Kota. Someone is going to hear us. We have to be stealthy. We have to be—"

I turn into the apartment and freeze. Kota is standing in the middle of the room with a hand over his mouth.

But it is not his hand.

"Don't move," a man says, holding a knife above Kota's head. "Don't move at all."

Chapter 20

Kota's wide eyes dart between me and the knife. I can feel his soul begging me to save him, but I'm not sure what to do. Instinctively, my hand moves toward my hatchet.

"Don't. Move," the man orders again, firmer this time. "I don't want to hurt you, but I will if I have to."

He shuffles to the left, dragging Kota with him as he looks out behind me and toward the hallway. He is much taller than Kota, by at least two feet. His mouth is covered by a dark cloth, and his eyes are hiding under the shadow of the hood of his black sweatshirt. I can almost feel his strength as he continues to pull Kota.

"Is there anyone else with you?" he demands, eyes still focused on the entrance.

"No," I state, my hand still hovering above my hatchet. "It's just us."

"If you are lying . . ." His voice drifts off for a moment. "I will do what I must to protect myself."

"Same here," I say, my eyes locking on his.

For a moment, the three of us are quiet—so quiet that the only thing we can hear is Kota's deep but quick breaths.

I can't hesitate this time.

If I have an opportunity to throw the hatchet, I have to try. I have to.

"Take off your backpack and kick it to the side," the man instructs. "Slowly."

I keep my hand above the hatchet and arch my back so the backpack slides off my shoulders and onto the floor.

Throw it, Aurora. Throw it!

"Drop that weapon too," he commands. "Push it all to the side."

I hesitate as the fear paralyzes my body.

Come on, Aurora! Throw it!

"Drop it now! NOW!" he yells.

Before I can fight with myself again, my hand releases the hatchet, and it drops next to the backpack. I push them both to the side as guilt floods my body. Once again, I failed to protect myself, and maybe Kota too.

"Okay, now listen closely," the man starts. "I am going to release him, but if either of you go anywhere near the bag or that axe—"

"I won't," I interrupt.

"Let me finish," he says, slowly lowering the knife to his side. "If you even *try* to grab it, I will do what I need to do."

I nod, and the man releases Kota, who runs over and wraps his arms around my waist. The man holds up a hand, as if he is surrendering, then slides the knife into a sheath on the side of his leg.

"We are going to take this slow, got it?" he says, one hand still extended outward. "Go sit over there."

He motions to the couch, which is against the wall. Kota and I walk backward until we bump into it, with Kota still holding on to me.

The man grabs the lone wooden chair to his left and drags it to the center of the room. Lowering himself into the seat, he pulls a small cloth from his pocket and wipes it slowly across his forehead, then brings his hood farther forward to cover his draping hair.

"Do you live in the building?" he asks.

"No," I respond.

"What about him?" He gestures to Kota.

"No, neither of us are from here," I add.

The man furrows his eyebrows as if I have offended him, and his tone changes to match it.

"How did you get to the city, then?" he asks, pointing to the window behind him. "Where are you from?"

"We got here yesterday, by boat."

"You have a boat?" the man says, shifting to the front of the chair. "Where is it?!"

"We *had* a boat," Kota corrects, his voice muffled by my jacket sleeve. "Someone stole it."

“Ugh,” the man says to himself as he relaxes back into his chair. “Nothing lasts more than a minute out here before it’s taken.”

He pauses for a second, then shakes his head.

“I’m going into the kitchen,” he informs us. “Don’t. Move.”

He walks over to my backpack and hatchet and, instead of picking them up, drags them to the other end of the room with his foot before disappearing.

“Let’s run,” Kota whispers, tugging on my sleeve. “We can make it.”

It’s tempting. The door is next to us, and we’d have a good head start. But we also have nowhere to go, and I don’t have anything to protect us with.

Maybe we could make it? Maybe we could get to another apartment and—

My thoughts are interrupted when the man returns with two cans.

“I’m assuming you are both hungry.” He gently lobs one of the cans toward us. Immediately Kota lets go of me and catches the can, rotating it quickly to read the label. There is a picture on the front of a pasta covered in red sauce.

“Here,” the man says, and tosses me an identical can. Then he throws us two spoons.

Kota looks at me like he is waiting for a release command. I peel the lid off of mine, and my mouth immediately waters at the sight of food. But I am not convinced, and the man notices.

"It's okay," he reassures me, pulling a third can from his back pocket. "Watch."

He pops the lid off of his can and dives in with his spoon, taking a big bite.

"See?" he says. "It's safe."

I dip my spoon into the mixture and put it in my mouth. Kota does too.

The food is cold but tastes better than anything I've eaten in days.

"Thank you," I say between bites. "We've been eating pumpkin pie mix for the last day."

"Yeah, I tried that once." The man chuckles slightly. "Couldn't get on board. Too pasty."

I can sense the atmosphere in the room shifting from threatening to almost friendly. Maybe it's because he looks oddly familiar. There's something about his eyes that pulls me in to want to know more. Still, I do not fully trust him, especially since I can't see his entire face.

"Don't worry, I've got plenty more food in the back if you want more," he says nonchalantly as he rolls up his sleeves. "Been collecting it from various places for a while."

"So, you're from the city?" I ask, scooping out yet another bite.

"Yeah, this building, actually. Lived here most of my adult life," he answers from behind the cloth mask. "But before we go any further, I should probably know your names."

"Kota," Kota says through a mouthful of ravioli.

"Aurora," I tag on.

"Nice to meet you," the man says, removing his hood and cloth bandana to reveal his full face. "My name is Markell."

I drop my spoon, sending the sauce-covered noodles bouncing off my leg and onto the floor.

The image of the picture-perfect family from the previous apartment comes into my mind. His features are strikingly similar to the man in the photo, with the exception of his beard and the sad expression on his face.

"I'm sorry," I say, picking the spoon up off the floor. "You said *Markell*?"

"Yeah, why?" he asks, scratching his now-visible gray beard. "You know me or something?"

"I think so, yes," I say. "Well, I don't *know* you, but I know you live in a room just below here. And that you have a family and—"

Markell leaps to his feet, knife in hand, and gets uncomfortably close to me.

"What do you know about my family?!" he yells, pointing the tip of the blade at my face.

Kota stops eating and tries to sink deep into the cushions of the sofa.

"I don't mean it like that!" I yell back, turning my face to avoid the knife. "We slept in an apartment downstairs last night, and there was a picture—a letter!—signed by someone named Markell."

Markell breathes heavily as he towers over me and Kota, assessing my words.

"If you are lying," Markell starts, aiming the knife closer to my face. "If you are with one of those looter groups trying to fool me—"

"We're not!" Kota interjects. "Promise!"

Markell's eyes flicker between Kota and me, his gaze sharp but weary. With a heavy sigh, he steps back, places the knife in the sheath, and sinks into the chair, the weight of exhaustion seeming to press him down.

"I'm . . . I'm sorry," he sputters out. "I'm just on edge, that's all."

Kota is clearly confused and leans forward to catch my attention.

"What letter? What picture?" he asks. "What are you talking about?"

"I saw his family pictures in the apartment last night," I say, pointing to Markell as he continues to rub his face. "There was a letter there too."

Markell looks up, his eyes now full of tears.

For the first time since entering the room, I don't feel threatened.

"Wait. The letter said you were leaving," I point out. "Why are you still here?"

Markell bites down on his bottom lip, his eyes fluttering shut as if he's trying to block something out. His body trembles, as if the burden is too much to bear.

"My wife and kids were visiting family outside of the city when the rain started. I was stuck here for work and just assumed, probably like everyone else, that when the rain stopped, they'd come back," he sputters. "But it never stopped."

He continues to tremble as he moves both hands into the pockets of his sweatshirt.

"Within just a week of the flooding, people in the city turned on each other. There were riots, looting, fights . . . you couldn't go outside without the fear of getting hurt, so I stayed in the apartment. Most people here either left or were forced to leave when the fighting started, but I've stayed hidden. I've got multiple rooms I spend time in while I wait for my luck to change."

"I'm so sorry," I say. "But your letter said you were leaving in a canoe. Why not just take it and go?"

"I've tried many times to get it, but it's in the storage area on the second floor, which is almost completely underwater," he explains, then pauses as he closes his eyes. "There is an exterior window above the water in that room, but I'm too big to go through it. Even if I was small enough, I'm not sure I could get the canoe out since the door to the fire escape is locked, so I have no way to leave and try to find my family or get to The Hill."

"You know how to get to The Hill?" Kota asks.

"Wait." Markell hesitates. "You know about The Hill too?"

"Sort of," I reply. "We have a map. It's in my bag."

"I only heard about it through one or two rumors," Markell states as he stands up and walks over to my backpack. "I'm assuming you know them both?"

"What do you mean, *both*?" Kota asks.

Markell digs through the contents of my bag.

"Well, if you are trying to get to The Hill, you must've heard it's a place of safety, a high ground with resources. Right?"

"We didn't hear anything," I admit. "I just know some people who might have planned to go there, I think. Oh, and from the map, of course."

As if on cue, Markell pulls the map from my bag. He unfurls it carefully, smooths the edges, and presses it flat against the floor. His finger traces the red line, following its path with a focused intensity, as if each inch could hold the answers we're all searching for.

"What is the other rumor, then?" Kota asks. "You said there was more than one?"

Markell looks up from the floor, then back down at the map.

"Another guy in this building had a two-way radio we listened to once the people in the city imploded on themselves. We heard chatter of people going there, but we also heard talk of people wanting to avoid it."

"Why would they avoid it if it's a place of safety?" I ask.

Markell hits me with a question I have wondered about but didn't want to consider.

"Do you *know* it's safe?"

Flashes of the water tower graffiti come into my brain.

"*Stand with The Hill, or do not stand at all,*" I mutter.

"What did you say?" Markell asks, breaking my trance.

"Stand with The Hill, or do not stand at all," Kota repeats. "We saw it on a water tower when we were traveling in the boat. Do you know that it means?"

Markell folds the map back up and places it in the bag.

"I don't know what that means exactly," he says, "but it doesn't sound inviting."

A giant thunderbolt erupts outside, and Markell runs to the living room window.

A second clap of thunder hits, this time shaking the apartment.

"When the thunder is that loud, it means the heart of the storm is right above us," Kota says, almost boastfully. "I learned that in Scouts."

"Oh, that's not thunder," Markell says, turning back to us. "Those are explosions."

Chapter 21

Kota stands up and joins Markell, quickly pressing his face into the center of the window. Another explosion rocks the apartment, and I struggle to maintain my footing as I make my way over to them.

"Where is it coming from?!" I ask. "I don't see anything."

"Over there," Markell points out. "Do you see the smoke?"

Across the city, between two very large structures, is a single trail of smoke weaving its way up toward the sky as it fights the ensuing rain.

"This is the most I've heard in a while," Markell informs us as we continue to gaze out the window. "I'm not sure if it's artillery, or maybe gas lines exploding, or—"

We are interrupted by a fourth explosion, one so strong it sends the three of us to the floor. Kota is the first one back to his feet.

"Oh my gosh! It's fire!"

Markell and I stand up next to Kota, taking in the

view of the growing flames outside. Despite the rain, which seems to have calmed to a drizzle, flames are shooting out the bottom of a building a few blocks ahead. But the flames don't stop there.

They are on the water too.

"No, no, no!" Markell shouts. "All the chemicals floating on this water!"

It's equal parts terrifying and incredible. The fire is dancing across the water like a living thing, its reflection splitting into jagged fragments on the rippling waves as it drifts and twists with the current through the heart of the city. Just when I think the fire is about to die off in the water, it jumps from the slick patches of floating oil to the framework of other buildings, where it climbs.

"Look at that!" Kota exclaims as another building a few blocks away is quickly engulfed in flames and dark smoke. "I hope there aren't people in there."

Suddenly, a window is pushed out from the building, just a floor above the flaming water. Two figures appear holding something I can't quite make out, but it's large. They heave it out of the building, and it splashes below, sending up waves that fling the nearby flames skyward. The first person positions themselves in the frame of the large window.

Don't do it! You aren't going to make it!

The person leaps forward and disappears into the water before their head pops back up just in front of the floating object. The second figure appears in the window, and they, too, jump out, landing directly on the object.

"They made it!" Kota shouts.

Another window breaks, this time a few more floors above the last. Then, my eye catches movement from a yellow brick building next to it, where multiple people are emerging from their windows.

"The fire must be worse than it appears from here," Markell suggests, pointing again at the smoke building behind the towering buildings. "The whole city must be catching fire!"

People are now spilling out from shattered windows and broken balconies as their screams cut through the crackle of flames. Some jump into the black water below—only to realize too late it's laced with fiery slicks of oil and chemicals, burning like molten veins around them as they thrash through the water.

Other people are clinging to makeshift rafts: doors, chairs, anything that floats—paddling away from the blaze that is continuing to make its way through the city. I want to move, to do something, but my legs feel rooted to the spot, paralyzed by the nightmare playing out before us.

"The fire is coming this way!" Kota says, tugging on my jacket. "What do we do?!"

"I have a plan!" Markell hollers as he runs toward the kitchen. "Quick, grab your stuff!"

Even though I don't really know Markell, his

announcement of a plan makes it clear we are together, at least for now, and since I don't have a plan of my own, I follow him. Kota sprints ahead and disappears into the kitchen as I grab my backpack from the ground, but my hatchet isn't there.

I look up to scan the floor to see where it might have gone, and I see Markell holding the hatchet, extending it in my direction.

"Can you actually use this?" he asks with purpose in his voice. "Could you have hit me with it?"

I nod yes before I can formulate any words.

"If there *is* danger outside, don't hesitate to use it," he says, shaking the hatchet. "You might not get another chance. And that is all we need to make it out of here right now. A chance!"

He flips the hatchet so the handle is facing me. My eyes remain locked on his as I take it from his grasp and put it the holster.

A chance. All we need is a chance.

Markell pivots, reenters the kitchen, and pulls a large orange duffel bag off the floor.

"Grab as much as you can!" he shouts, pointing to the cabinets lined with cans of food. "We're going to try and get to my canoe before the fire gets here."

I pause. "But you said you can't get to—"

"I know what I said! Just trust me!"

I yank open my backpack and shove it against the edge of the nearest cabinet. Not sparing a single glance at the labels on the cans, I thrust my arm across the shelf in one sweeping motion, sending cans tumbling in all directions. A chaotic clatter fills the room as some crash to the floor, but half land inside my bag, rattling as they pile in.

I zip the backpack shut and spin around to see Markell and Kota doing the same. I don't even bother asking where Kota's backpack came from as we heave the heavy bags over our shoulders and follow Markell into the living room.

"I can only think of a single option right now," he says, eyes wide and intense. "We need to get to my canoe, and I think one of you can reach it."

Before I can respond, Markell yanks open the door and takes off down the hallway. I sling the other backpack strap over my shoulder and run after him as more explosions rock the floorboards beneath my feet.

"This way!" Markell orders as we reach the end of the hallway. "We'll use the fire escape!"

My body is on autopilot as we follow Markell out the window and onto the landing of the steel fire escape. We are on the opposite side of the building now, and even though I can't see the flames anymore, the smell of smoke and chemicals is strong enough to make me feel like I am in them.

"Hurry!" Markell urges as we move down the first of three ladders below.

"You can do it!" I yell to Kota, who is just ahead of me but moving as slowly as I am.

The backpack weighs me down, and the straps dig deep into my shoulder, making it difficult to navigate each step as the clanging of our frantic feet hitting the metal ladder fills the air. The sound is quickly overtaken by the screams of people off in the distance, though. Their words are indistinguishable, but the panicked shouting is clear and growing louder by the second.

We finally get to the last landing of the fire escape, hovering just a few feet above the water. Now that we are closer, I can see the floating, discolored swirls, and the smell is even worse—sharp and acidic, like burnt plastic mixed with gasoline. It clings to my nose and throat. Even the air above the surface feels heavy, like it's carrying the weight of something dying.

"That's the oil," Markell says, pointing at the blobs in the water. "I'm hoping it's not inside too!"

He turns toward the building and begins to kick in a small, wire-covered window. It only takes a few attempts before the window caves inward, splashing into the water inside.

"The canoe is in there," Markell says, pointing to the black abyss inside the building. "I can't get through the window, but if one of you can, I think you can unlock the door and shove the canoe through!"

Another explosion resonates in the distance, followed by more screams.

"Neither of you will fit!" Kota yells over the noise.

"Right? I think I am the only one who is small enough to slip through."

Things are moving too quickly for me to stop Kota, and before I can muster a word, he sheds his backpack, jacket, and undershirt, and hands them each to Markell.

"No, Kota, don't! What about the chemicals in the water? What if—" I stop talking while I try to remove my own backpack, but then I come up with a new idea. "I'll do it!"

"You won't fit!" Markell says, speaking my thoughts. "We don't have time to argue!"

Kota is down to just his underwear. He looks even younger now, and weaker too. The lack of food has taken a toll on his body, and I can see the faint outline of his rib cage.

"You don't have to do this!" I yell above the screams around us. "We can find another way to—"

"If there were another way," Markell interrupts, "I would've found it by now. This is our chance. We *have* to take it!"

Another explosion erupts somewhere behind us, causing the metal of the fire escape to squeal as vibrations run through it.

There isn't another option. It has to be Kota.

"At least take this!" I say, yanking the flashlight from the back pocket of Kota's pants and pressing it into his hand. He clicks it on without hesitation and clenches it between his teeth. Without another word, he sits down on the edge of the fire escape and lowers his legs directly into the open window.

Markell drops his duffel bag, shoves the clothes in it, then grabs Kota's hands, lowering him the rest of the way until he disappears beneath the frame of the window.

"Are you okay?!" I yell into the dark chamber. "What do you see?"

"My feet can't touch the bottom, and there's a lot of stuff floating around in here," Kota announces. "It's hard to see far ahead."

A few seconds go by, and Markell calls out.

"Do you see anything yet?" he asks.

Silence.

"Kota?!" I yell. "Can you hear us?"

I can only see the occasional beam of Kota's flashlight as both Markell and I peer through the small window.

He will make it! He has to!

A sudden scream diverts my attention. Between the gaps of burning oil slicks directly behind us, there is a mattress floating down the river directly behind us with two people on top of it, fighting violently.

The larger of the two throws the smaller one into the water, creating a splash that sends ripples through the patches of contamination. Flames skitter across the top, merging the oil slicks together until the entire surface of the water is on fire around him.

The man spins around quickly in the water to

grab the mattress, but with no success. He is met with a foot to the face as he is kicked farther away from the floating refuge, and he disappears into the flaming water.

Markell puts an arm in front of me for protection as the other man and mattress float by. The three of us stare at each other, as if each one of us is waiting for the other to make a move. He crouches, steadying himself on the mattress as the current of the water pulls him past us and around the corner of the building.

"I found it!" a voice echoes behind us. "I found the canoe!"

We turn to see Kota, whose face is barely visible in the window as the flashlight illuminates the dark water around him. He swims toward us, pulling the canoe with him.

"Can you unlock the door?!" Markell yells quickly as he braces his hands against the window. "Then I can help!"

"I'll try!" Kota whimpers. "The water is so cold . . . I'm . . . I'm losing my breath!"

"Quickly!" Markell demands. "Then we can pull you and the canoe through!"

"No!" I interject, leaning over the railing so Kota can hear me better. "He isn't going to make it! We need to get him out through the window!"

Kota takes a deep breath and then, without any warning, dives underwater.

Before I can make a move, his head pops back up.

"Wait! I think I unlocked it!" Kota yells. "But I can't open the door. It's stuck!"

A large, metallic groaning overtakes the conversation as Markell and I spin back around. The yellow brick building a few blocks away is teetering as poles and iron snap like twigs under the buckling pressure. Then, in a quick, thunderous roar, the top of the building gives way, crashing into the fiery water below. The impact shatters the wall of the building next to it, sending a smattering of debris into the air.

"Hold on!" Markell yells as a giant wave of water begins to radiate from the epicenter of the fall.

"*No!* Kota!" I scream.

It's too late. The wave of water cascades down the flooded street, raising the water feet above where it stood just moments ago. Formerly submerged cars begin to rise and roll over each other like sand on the beach, bumping into the other buildings as they pass.

"Go up!" yells Markell, who is already a ladder above me.

I climb further and reach toward his hand just as the water begins to hit my feet. Once our fingers connect, he hoists me up effortlessly as the wave consumes the landing beneath us, swallowing the entrance to the storage area.

I watch as the wave of fiery debris passes and rushes between the rest of the buildings, overtaking the dozens of people who thought they were safe on their floating creations.

They didn't stand a chance.

The wave fully passes, revealing the landing, which now has shards of wood and metal jammed in its links, along with our backpacks and bags.

"Back down!" Markell declares. He yanks my sleeve before skipping the ladder and jumping to the landing below. He takes his sweatshirt off and, without any hesitation, dives into the thick water.

I glance back at the collapsed building. A second ripple surges forward, its crest climbing higher with each passing second, causing multiple patches of fiery oil slicks to merge together. I scramble up the ladder again, gripping the railing as the wave crashes into the wall and fire escape, sending a bone-rattling jolt through the entire structure.

As soon as it passes, I leap down to the landing again, scanning the debris for any trace of Markell and Kota.

Seconds go by.

My heart pounds.

Come on, Markell. Find him!

The surface of the water bubbles, and a giant green object breaches the top.

The canoe!

It extends a few more feet into the air before slamming back to the water, spitting oily chunks in all directions. I grasp the railing of the fire escape and lean out over the water, latching one hand to the side of the now fully visible canoe.

"She's got a boat!" a voice screams above the aching groans of the collapsing city. "Grab it!"

Three people emerge from a window across the street. Their arms flail in desperation as they jump into the open spaces between the flaming globs of water below and swim in my direction.

No! Not now!

With a final, desperate yank, I drag the canoe closer. Flames begin to claw across the water's surface toward me, and the heat presses against my back as I snatch Markell's and Kota's bags, hurling them into the canoe before another wave takes them.

Markell's head appears above the water, and he gasps for air.

"I'm right here!" I yell. "Take my hand!"

But he doesn't. Instead, he takes one deep inhale and disappears back into the water.

I glance at the swimmers. Somehow, they've managed to avoid the burning wreckage of twisted metal and splintered wood and are already halfway across the flooded street.

The sight is surreal, like something out of a nightmare.

When I turn back, Markell breaks the surface again, gasping for air, one hand already gripping the railing. He's moving with urgency, but before I can warn him about the approaching people, he dips his other arm deeper into the water, pulling something up.

Kota!

Relief washes over me—until I see his face. His mouth is slack, his eyes closed, and his limbs dangle lifelessly in the water.

"Get him in the canoe!" Markell yells, snapping me into action. I grab Kota's floating arms and brace myself against the fire escape as I pull with every ounce of strength I have. The water fights me, but I don't let go. Inch by inch, I drag him onto the platform, my arms burning with the effort.

Markell hauls himself out beside me, wasting no time as he maneuvers the canoe against the railing where Kota lies. His movements are quick and focused despite the chaos and fire swirling toward us.

"Go!" he shouts, scooping Kota into his arms.

Without thinking, I leap into the canoe, my knees stinging as I hit the base of it. I fumble and try to stand to receive Kota, but Markell is already placing him into the front of the canoe.

Suddenly, a hand shoots out of the water, locking around Markell's ankle in a viselike grip. With a big *yank,* his body slams chest-first onto the perforated metal platform of the fire escape. The impact knocks the wind from his lungs, and he gasps for air.

The hand releases Markell's ankle, and a man begins to emerge from the water. He clings to the opposite side of the fire escape, his face a grotesque mask of blood and bruises highlighted by the flames around us. His eyes are wild, filled with desperation and rage.

With a grunt, the man hauls himself out of the water, every muscle trembling from the effort. The metal groans beneath the added weight as he drags one leg over the edge, then the other, inching closer to Markell with every breath.

Markell twists around onto his back and delivers a swift, forceful kick directly into the belly of the attacker, sending him sailing into the hard rail behind him as two more men pull themselves onto the platform.

"Get in the boat!" I scream.

Markell scrambles to his feet and positions himself just in front of the canoe, but then halts.

"Hurry," I plead. "Get in!"

He turns around, his eyes widening as the two men draw nearer. Their movements are slow but deliberate, aligning themselves shoulder to shoulder with the first man as they help him up. Together, all three men form a wall of terrifying expressions as their shoulders heave up and down with each breath.

A chance. We need a chance!

I grab the hatchet from my hip and raise it into the air. The men pause at the sight.

I can do this! Throw it, Aurora! Throw it!

"Markell, move!" I scream, but he doesn't.

Everything slows down. The flicker of the flames.

The forward steps of the attackers. The bricks dropping from the toppling buildings around us.

I lock eyes with Markell, and he looks at me with an expression I have not seen before: a deep, melancholy gaze that takes me in and almost makes me forget about the situation surrounding us.

In one swift action, Markell's hand latches on to the stern of the canoe. For a split second, I think he's about to jump in, but instead, he pushes with all his strength, launching the canoe forward. The force shoots the canoe away from the fire escape, cutting through the water and putting distance between us and the mayhem in an instant.

"No!" I scream, but it is too late.

Markell turns around just in time to dodge a punch from the man on his left, but his jaw is caught by a second one that sends him reeling backward. Still, he recovers and lunges forward, pushing the man back into the others as he begins to throw punches of his own.

The whole scene is chaos—the roar of the fiery waves, the crashing of debris, the distant shouts of others caught in the madness—but Markell is still fighting. Against all odds, he's still fighting.

He's fighting for us.

He's giving us a chance!

I glance down at Kota, whose lips are turning a pale blue.

"Kota!" I yell, patting his face to try to wake him

up. He doesn't respond, so I tilt his chin back, seal my mouth over his, and force a breath into his lungs, just like Jada taught me. It's the only thing I can think to do.

His body stays limp, so I lock my elbows and drive my palms into his chest, one push after another, counting in my head.

Twenty-one, twenty-two, twenty-three . . .

Come on, Kota! Please!

Thirty-six, thirty-seven, thirty-eight . . .

On "thirty-nine," Kota spurts to life, coughs up a dark liquid, and gasps for air.

"Kota!" I cheer. "I've got you!"

The waves rock the canoe. I put my hands around Kota's face, his eyes darting around to take it all in. I look back up just as a giant orange flame rolls across the water, obscuring the fight between Markell and the rest of the men.

We can't go back.

Another large wave rolls underneath the canoe and pushes us past the perimeter of the city and out into the vast ocean of water. The flames continue to climb higher on the towering buildings behind us, casting the entire city in an orange glow.

I can't see Markell anymore.

He's gone.

Chapter 22

We are not alone.

As the fire rages through the buildings, sending black pillars of smoke across the sky, people continue to emerge, but not by choice.

Some are jumping out of burning buildings and into the swaths of oil and fiery water below, while others are attempting to climb on smoking wreckage that spills out in droves from the center of the city, like a conveyer belt of trash in an incinerator.

One woman bursts through the water's surface, about a hundred yards away, gasping like she's been underwater for hours. The waves from the collapsing city don't give her a chance to breathe—they slam into her, dragging her under again until she fights her way back up. Her arms thrash wildly, and it's clear she's barely holding on. The current is relentless, tugging at her, pulling her deeper with each surge.

I can help! I can save her!

"Over here!" I yell, waving my arms to get her attention. "Swim this way!"

Her face twists in panic, eyes darting around as if searching for something—anything—to grab onto. Debris floats past, but she's too busy trying to stay above the surface to reach for it. Then a plank drifts close by, and she lunges for it, her fingers nearly slipping before they lock around it.

"You can do it!" I scream. "This way!"

For a moment, she clings to the plank there, water streaming down her face.

But as quickly as the woman emerged, she drops into a growing abyss beneath her as wood and debris topple into the black circle.

A Dark Pool!

I scan the canoe for anything that can help me paddle. To my complete surprise, there is an oar latched to the inside wall.

I wrench the oar free from the wall next to Kota, who is still coughing, and paddle frantically away from the smoldering city. Each inhale burns my lungs, and I realize how hazy the air around me has become, obscuring my vision and making it almost impossible to see ahead. Large flakes of white fall, like giant snowflakes from a snowstorm.

But it isn't snow.

Dense ash begins to accumulate on the rim of the canoe and the top of my hood.

Mixed with the drops of rain, it thickens to a

dark-gray sludge that sticks to me like a papier-mâché project.

I paddle hard for a full minute until my lungs can't take it anymore. The scorching pain in my chest becomes too much to bear, and I collapse on my back next to Kota in the center of the canoe.

I slow my breathing to fend off the coughing, but it's impossible. The air is so thick with smoke and ash, it's as if I'm engulfed in the fire itself.

"Aurora? Markell?" Kota asks, coughing between names. "Are you there?"

I reach out to touch him; my eyes flicker from the lack of oxygen in the air.

Is this how it ends? Did Markell protect us for nothing?

My breathing becomes shallower until I feel like I am not breathing at all. My eyes no longer flicker but instead see patches of black and bright light, like I am pacing in and out of a dreamscape.

I have no idea how long it has been. I can't piece together a single coherent thought as the remaining light is slowly overtaken by darkness.

I wake to a chill tracing its way across my face.

It starts off as a whisper, just a faint sparkle of cold that runs across my cheek, over my nose, and up into my hair.

The chill comes again, this time more powerful,

catching strands of hair and pulling them across my face.

It's the wind.

I am too weak to sit up, but I strain my eyes to focus on the sky above me. Dark smoke is swirling in wisps, each twisting and stretching upward before dissolving into the cool air. As the wind crescendos, the coolness begs my body to take in oxygen, and I gasp as my lungs are met with the cleanest, purest air I've had in a while. It's not perfect, but it will do. It catches me off guard, and I almost choke as my body attempts to consume more.

"Aurora?" Kota calls. "Are you there?"

I reach out until I find Kota's hand and squeeze it, slowly regaining control of my body. The fresh oxygen fills my lungs.

"I'm . . . I'm sorry I couldn't protect you," I stammer, still holding Kota's hand. "I should have been in the water. I should have thrown the hatchet! I should've—"

Kota squeezes my hand back as we lie motionless next to each other on the floor of the canoe. I am not sure what he is thinking, although the fact that we are holding hands must mean he isn't upset with me. But I am.

I said I would protect him.

I didn't.

I *couldn't.*

The wind continues to push the smoke farther

and farther out of view until all that's left in the sky are the dark rain clouds above, which are a welcome sight after being engulfed by the smoke from the city. When I finally sit up, I can see a giant cloud of ash hovering above the water as the wind guides it away from us.

A single ray of sunlight stretches over the horizon, slipping through the mist and casting a dull glow inside the boat. My head throbs, my muscles ache, and for a moment, I can't tell if I'm still dreaming. I thought I'd only closed my eyes for a moment, but the shifting light, the stillness of the water, and the ache in my limbs tell me otherwise.

We've been drifting all night.

Kota sits up, too, and I see that he still doesn't have any clothes on.

"Oh my gosh!" I say, unzipping Markell's orange duffel bag. "Get these on, quick!"

I reach into the bag and feel around for Kota's clothes, which are fairly dry. I hand him everything, and he wastes no time getting them on, his body trembling.

"How long—" Kota begins, but he is interrupted by his own deep, dry cough.

"Slow down," I say as I try to assess his health. "You almost drowned."

I pull Kota's shivering frame against my chest and wrap my arms around him. I rub my hands briskly along his sides, trying to chase the chill from his body as he leans into me, his cough rattling both of us. Desperate for any bit of warmth, I shift us toward the lone ray of sunlight stretching across the water. I can't see the sun rising, but I can feel its faint heat, and I hope Kota can too.

As the minutes drag on, Kota's cough lessens, and his shaking dispels into occasional shivers. I wait a bit longer before letting him go, then turn him around to better assess him.

"I drowned?" Kota asks, his energy perking up a little. "The last thing I remember . . . The last thing I remember is unlocking the door underwater."

"Well, you saved us," I say, putting my hand on his shoulder for comfort. "You were so brave."

"Wait," he says, as he pulls his hood over his wet hair. "Where is Markell? Is he in another canoe?"

"Markell . . . didn't make it," I inform him.

Kota pulls his legs close to his chest and rests his head between his knees.

"But I found the canoe," he says. "We were all gonna make it out together."

I put my hand on Kota's knee and try to catch his gaze.

"You did so amazing," I said. "You did everything you could do to give us a chance, and that's what Markell did. He gave us—he gave us a chance."

"But he deserves a chance, too, doesn't he? To be with his family?" Kota asks.

He did have a chance, though.

I could have thrown the hatchet.

Markell knew that!

Why did he decide to save us instead?

Before I can respond, the canoe bumps into something beneath the water. I grab the oar just as the object in front of us comes into view.

It's the top of a tree.

The canoe brushes against a floating branch as more trees seem to rise out of the water. Some only have the tops showing, making it seem like a nursery of baby pines, but others are shooting farther up out of the water—three, even four feet—their branches sending ripples through the water as the current pushes between them.

"Is this the forest we were hoping to find?" I ask Kota as a flicker of hope resurges.

Kota is already opening my backpack, and he pulls out the map.

"I'm not sure," he admits, looking at his compass.

I glance behind us and see the trail of dark smoke still being pushed through the air. Although the wind has carried the smoke away from us, I can trace the trail until it peaks at a small collection in the distance.

Kota glances back and forth between the map, smoke trail, and the seemingly growing forest ahead.

"I'm so tired," Kota continues, resting his head between his knees as he coughs, "and so cold and—"

Kota erupts in a series of heavy, body-shaking

coughs. The span between them is so short, he can barely get a single breath, and he has to brace himself to stay upright.

"I've got you," I say, pulling him until his back is against me. "Just breathe with me. You can do it."

I exaggerate my breathing in deep, slow movements until Kota is able to match it. We sit together for a few more minutes before I turn him around again.

"You need to rest, Kota," I say. "I'm sorry I tried to get you to read the map right away. Here, just lie down."

I help Kota recline against the back of the canoe and then look at the trees as the current guides us into the forest. After only being surrounded by buildings, being thrust into a vast natural landscape feels otherworldly.

Did Jada and Niko go through here? Were they able to avoid the city?

As more questions about Niko and Jada swirl in my brain, I realize I don't even need to paddle, at the rate we are going. Instead, I guide the canoe with careful precision, using the oar to push off the trunks of submerged trees while we glide past their rough bark. With each gentle nudge, I navigate around low-hanging branches that stretch over the water, pushing their tangled limbs out of the way. Each time I do, a wave of fresh pine fills the air, and I'm surprised how crisp and invigorating it feels to take in such clean air.

I wish Kota could smell it, but I don't want to bother him. He is asleep in the back of the canoe, and it seems like half the day goes by before he opens his eyes again.

"Aurora, where are we now?" he asks between coughs as his eyes scan the trees. "How long have I been asleep?"

"I have no idea," I say, pushing another branch out of our way. "It's been a long time, though."

Kota sits up groggily, then rummages through Markell's duffel bag until he pulls out a single can. He quickly pops off the top and dives his hands into the contents.

"Pears," he says, barely audible through his coughing. "Want some?"

I smile and reach out to the take the can, but an object in the trees halts my action.

Between the overlapping branches just behind Kota is a large, white piece of wood, nailed to the trunk of a tree. As the canoe moves forward, I am able to get a better view, revealing bold, jagged letters slashed in vibrant red across the stark white of the wood.

STAND WITH THE HILL
OR DO NOT STAND AT ALL.

Kota turns to see what I am staring at and says what I am thinking.

"Are we positive we still want to go there? Markell didn't seem so sure."

"If The Hill is anything like the city, then no, we shouldn't go," I state as I take in the words of the sign. "But I don't know what other choice we have. Where else would we go?"

"But what if The Hill is full of attackers?" Kota asks, turning back to get my attention. "They'll take our stuff, just like they did in the city! Or worse!"

Nothing Kota is saying is wrong. Going to The Hill could turn out to be the worst possible decision. But it could also be the decision that saves our lives.

I look down at Markell's orange bag that sits between Kota and me.

Markell . . .

Markell wasn't like those attackers, though.

He helped us. He actually helped us.

That should be the focus. There must be other helpers out there. There have to be.

"Hey," I gently say to Kota, tapping his knee. "We can't think that way. There are still good people out there. There must be, because Markell was one of them."

Kota looks at me like he is longing for a better answer.

"But we're the good people, too, right?" he asks, his eyes scanning mine.

"We are," I confirm. "We are the good guys. Now, can I have a bite of that?"

Kota hands me the can, and I sink my teeth into the most delicious food I've had in recent memory. As I close my eyes to take in the flavors of the sweet pears, I envision the two of us in a home, seated around a fire, laughing and playing games while we eat gobs of candy.

Markell didn't give his life for nothing.

He gave us a chance.

Kota and I have to survive—we *will* survive.

All we can do now is hope there are more people like Markell waiting for us ahead.

Chapter 23

There is a quiet rhythm as we slice through the water between the treetops, and the forest feels alive. Even though the rain is still coming down softly, small, occasional rays of light filter through the branches, casting shifting patterns on the surface, but the stillness of it all is unnerving. Around us, the air seems to hum with the faint buzz of insects as small ripples break the top of the water, hinting at life below too.

"Do you think we can fish here, Kota?" I ask, pointing at the ripples on the water. "I think the fish are biting."

"If we had any line to fish with, then maybe," he says as he opens another unlabeled can of food. "Hey, I think this one is peaches!"

I haven't taken inventory of our food, but it seems like we have enough to easily last us a week. Markell's bag is full to the top, and mine is equally packed. Even though most of the cans are missing labels, I'll take my chances with mystery meals over choking down slimy fish—if we could even catch one, that is.

Kota hands me a can, and I'm lucky enough to get the same thing: peaches. I sip the sugary liquid.

"Ewwww," Kota says. "You like doing that?"

"I like it a lot more than raw fish," I say while raising the can to him in a cheers motion. "Don't knock it until you try it."

Kota curls his lip upward, then shrugs and takes a sip at the same time I do.

"Hey, that's actually pretty good," he says in a childlike voice, then goes back for another swig. "I hope the rest of the cans are peaches too."

Even though Kota still looks extremely weak, the bounce in his voice makes it seem like he'll be okay, which makes my shoulders relax.

"As long as it isn't fish, I'll be happy," I joke.

Kota and I continue to eat as the canoe bumps between branches, funneling itself between the grasps of the pine trees. Every once in a while, I have to use the oar to lift a branch out of our way or over our heads, which Kota finds amusing. His occasional laughter is enough to keep my attitude positive, even though I'm stressed about what lies ahead.

"I wish I knew if we are headed in the right direction," I say while brushing my fingers against the slimy bark of a submerged branch. "This place is like a maze."

Kota has the map displayed directly in front of him on the back seat. He takes a minute to look at his compass before giving me the news.

"I know the forest comes before The Hill, but without seeing the elevation changes on the ground, it's hard to know where we are, or where we are going."

It's sobering, but I didn't expect a solid answer either. It seems the farther we travel, the more lost I feel, especially since the trees are becoming denser. Everything is surreal, like we're in a forgotten world that doesn't belong to us.

"Look!" Kota blurts out, pointing to a crooked treetop ahead. "Squirrels!"

To my disbelief, he is right. Two brown squirrels are perched on the very top of a pine tree, jockeying for position. As one claims the high ground, the other jumps on its back, sending them both tumbling down to the branches just above the water.

"Oh, cute!" Kota continues. "They are playing with each other!"

A third squirrel shows up to join the others.

"I don't think they're playing," I say as the three squirrels begin to bite and scratch each other. They get so entangled that they lose balance and all fall into the water, where they swim to different trees, only to then head back to the tallest one.

They are not just fighting for territory.

They are fighting for survival.

"I can't believe anything is still alive out here," I say to Kota as the squirrels engage in another match. Images of the deer from Niko and Jada's neighborhood come to mind, and I shudder, thinking about how I had to crawl over it to get in the boat when I escaped.

Kota doesn't say anything for a moment, seemingly taking in the thought of all the animals that were lost to the flood, but then he surprises me.

"If they weren't fighting, they could each have a tree to themselves," he says, gesturing to the other trees. "They are just like the attackers in the city."

His comment is more than accurate; it's poignant. Why aren't more people helping each other, like Markell helped us? Why are so many people so desperate to take from others instead of teaming up to figure out a solution?

As the squirrels continue their tussle, I flash back to when I was sitting in the mansion, watching the man struggle to get in the aluminum boat.

Niko said we shouldn't help him, but what if we had? Maybe he knew something that could have helped, or better yet, maybe we could have figured out something *together.*

We never gave him a chance, like Markell gave a chance to us.

Everyone deserves a chance. Everyone.

"Hey, do you hear that?" Kota asks, interrupting my thoughts. He points into the thick forest ahead. "Is that . . . screaming?"

I do hear it: a loud, wailing cry.

The noise dissipates quickly, but then returns with a more guttural tone.

"It doesn't sound like a person to me," I whisper, looking back at Kota. "Does it?"

Kota has his hands on either side of the canoe, like he is getting ready to jump. I motion with one hand to stay still as the piercing scream continues.

"There!" Kota shouts, the panic disappearing from his face. "Look at that!"

My gaze snaps to a low-hanging branch, where the silhouette of a large creature takes shape. It crouches as first, then shifts forward to perch almost perfectly still above the water as its deep, rumbling growl splits the sound of the rain.

"It's a bobcat!" Kota says, pointing, almost giddy with excitement. "I've never seen one in the wild before!"

The bobcat's sharp yellow eyes come into focus as it shifts its spotted body amid the gnarled branches of the trees. For a moment, not one of us moves, suspended in a strange, silent connection as Kota and I float by, just a few trees away.

Then its mouth opens, and a second deep, rumbling growl vibrates through the still air and small raindrops. The sound is low and menacing, like a warning that carries across the water. As we silently drift by, something catches my eye beneath the bobcat's feet.

It's another animal, or what used to be one.

"What is *that*?" Kota whispers, apparently seeing the same thing I do. "I can't tell."

I don't know how anyone could.

The mass of bones and flesh beneath the bobcat is unrecognizable. It breaks its gaze from us and begins to tear into the pile, ripping pieces of fur from the skin of its prey. It's a disgusting sight.

We float past the bobcat, and I have to pick up the oar to push the canoe away from the biggest tree I've seen so far. It's so thick I wouldn't be able to wrap my arms around it if I tried.

"Look up!" Kota announces, just in time for me to see another squirrel descend from a branch and drop right into the center of our canoe.

"Out!" I say as I try and slap the squirrel with my oar. "Get out of here!"

"What a silly guy!" Kota laughs, waving his arms to try and get it to move. "Why would it come in our canoe?"

Before I can answer, the sound of snapping branches above diverts my attention.

I don't have time to warn Kota before a second bobcat lands squarely on top of the squirrel, almost toppling the boat in the process. I launch myself to the opposite side of the canoe to keep it from tipping as a yowl erupts from the bobcat.

"Agh!" Kota screams as the bobcat skids on the base of the canoe, its claws scratching for traction. The squirrel evades a swipe from the predator and makes a flying leap to a branch just behind Kota, leaving the bobcat and Kota face-to-face.

What do I do?!

Last time, I couldn't protect him. I just watched. Helpless. Weak. And he almost didn't make it.

Not this time.

I grip the paddle so hard my fingers ache. My breath is shallow; my heart is slamming against my ribs. I have seconds—maybe less. I can't freeze. I can't let fear keep me still.

Not again.

"Aurora!" Kota begs as he presses backward as far as he can go. "Do something!"

Then, without warning, the bobcat lunges at Kota and releases a high-pitched *hiss* that rattles my eyes. Kota reacts in an instant, curling into a tight ball just as the bobcat pounces, its front and back legs locking around his back.

"*No!*" I yell as the canoe violently rocks side to side. My heartbeat crashes like thunder in my ears, drowning out everything but the sickening sound of snarls and growls. I can barely move as fear swiftly creeps in and locks my body in place.

But a familiar interior voice begins to rise above it all. It repeats, growing louder and louder by the second.

"If there is danger outside, don't hesitate to use it! You might not get another chance. And that is all we need to make it out of here right now. A chance!"

Markell's voice!

I grit my teeth, plant my feet, and force my arms

to move. My whole body protests as I swiftly raise the oar above my head like a sledgehammer. With a sharp inhale, I swing my arms forward with everything I have in me.

The blade of the oar finds its mark, its sharp, sloped side sinking down into the side of the bobcat. It flashes its teeth in agony and lets out a pained yowl as it releases Kota and turns to see what is causing so much pain.

I pull back, lifting the oar above my head for a second strike. The bobcat lets out another loud yowl and swings its powerful paw toward me. I tumble over.

Despite its open wound, the bobcat faces me: crouching, tail flicking, muscles coiled, ready for another strike.

Don't make me do it!

The bobcat hesitates, its ears twitching, eyes narrowing.

I can feel its desperation.

Then, with a low growl, it pounces toward me with its front claws extended.

But I am faster.

With one powerful side swing, the oar catches the bobcat in the side, sending it over the edge of the canoe and into the water.

There is an explosion of thrashing and splashing as the bobcat struggles to swim. It paddles toward the canoe, possibly assessing if it has the option to rejoin us, but I already have the oar in hand. With just two strong strokes, I steer us away from danger while the bobcat scrambles to the nearest tree.

I turn to see Kota, who is lying in the back of the boat, panting, with blood streaking his jacket.

I drop to my knees beside him, hands trembling. I check for the worst.

"It's okay," Kota says. "It's not my blood. I'm fine!"

I don't believe him, and frantically check his legs, arms, and back for any sign of injury.

He can't be hurt. He can't be hurt!

I must protect him! We will survive!

"Aurora!" Kota yells, trying to snap me out of my fixation. He tries to gently push me off. "I'm okay!"

Push! Breathe!

Survive!

I whip back around to check on the threat of the bobcat. Even with two large wounds, it has climbed partway up the tree. Its back rises and falls as it catches it breath.

"Aurora!" Kota yells again, grabbing my wrist. "You're bleeding!"

I glance down to see my hands tightly clasped around the oar, with rivulets of blood weaving trails between my knuckles. There's a gash in my jacket sleeve, a giant laceration across my upper arm.

My body shakes and twitches. Energy surges through me.

I think I am in shock.

Kota pushes his fingers into my hand and then

attempts to pry the oar from my grasp. It clangs on the canoe floor, and Kota wraps his arms around me, halting the tremors that are taking over my body.

I saved him. This time, I saved him.

The thought drifts through my mind, but the moment doesn't feel real yet, like it's hovering just outside of me, waiting to be ripped away. I'm bracing for the part where everything goes wrong. Where I miss my chance. Where I'm too slow, too weak, too helpless.

Because that's what always happens.

I see danger. I reach for the moment, the chance to stop it, to fix it—but it slips through my fingers. Just like before.

But not this time.

This time, I didn't fail.

And yet I can't shake the feeling that the world is holding its breath, waiting to correct itself, waiting to take something back from me. Because I don't get to win. I never have.

Not like this.

Not without some sort of cost.

"It's okay . . . it's okay," Kota repeats over and over, trying to bring me back. "Aurora, you saved me . . . you saved me . . . you saved me!"

Chapter 24

Kota helps me settle into the canoe. It tilts slightly before wedging itself between two trees. My gaze drops past my bloodied, trembling hand to the oar lying on the canoe's floor, its blade slick with blood.

My stomach turns.

"You don't look good," Kota announces as he rummages through my backpack. "You look like you're gonna be sick."

I fend off the wooziness by taking slow, deep breaths. I watch Kota pull out the IFAK. He moves quickly to pull out a large roll of gauze and tape.

"How bad is it?" I ask Kota. I painfully remove my rain jacket.

Kota stops unrolling the gauze, and my full injury comes into sight.

"Um . . ." Kota says. "Can you move it?"

I raise my arm until it is horizonal, which isn't as painful as I expected, and get my first good look. Across the side of my arm, near my bicep, are three giant rips into my skin, maybe a quarter inch deep.

"Let me cover it," Kota suggests, raising the bandage over my arm. "Don't look."

I take his advice and lift my head toward the sky, allowing the rain to hit my face. The cool drops provide relief as the fire of adrenaline pulses through my body, and I open my mouth in the hopes that this will help even more.

"There, I'm done," Kota announces. He shifts to sit next to me. "How do you feel?"

"I feel more nauseous than anything else," I state while sliding my rain jacket back on over the bandages. "I think the cut looks worse than it actually is, though."

This news seems to ease Kota, and he lets out a deep, relieved breath.

I can't believe I did it.

I stare at the bloodied end of the oar on the floor of the canoe. For some reason, the sight of it doesn't add any more discomfort to my turning stomach. I pick the oar up and turn it in my hands, watching as the rain erases the bloody proof, drop by drop, until it looks almost clean again. Almost like it never happened.

But the moment is still there, carved into me.

I feel . . . different.

The thought settles deeper, and even though my hands still shake and my heart still pounds, there's something growing within me too—something stronger.

"I haven't seen you do anything like that before," Kota says as he pulls his hood over his head.

"I didn't think I could, until just now," I admit.

There is a long pause as the rain patters against the canoe.

"How are you so brave?" Kota asks. "Were your parents that brave too?"

The last time Kota asked me about my family, my biological family, I was able to deflect the question. But for some reason, in this moment, it doesn't feel right to do that again. I want Kota to know who I am, which means he needs to know my past.

"I've never known my parents," I admit.

"You don't know anything about them?" Kota asks, not fully understanding the situation.

"No, not even their names," I continue. "My file only had the date when I was given to the foster center, which was apparently the day after I was born. Otherwise, I've lived in a lot of foster homes, and the last people I was living with were my foster parents, Niko and Jada."

Kota sits quietly, his face scanning mine like he is searching for something deeper.

"Do you think they're dead?" he finally asks. "Niko and Jada?"

"I don't know," I say as I take the oar and dislodge the canoe from between the two trees. "I woke up and they were gone. Just . . . gone."

Saying it out loud stings.

A ball forms in my throat as I take a slow breath, trying to keep my emotions in check. My face feels warm, and tears blur my vision, but I fight them off.

"Well, I will *never* leave you," Kota says, his eyes taking me in. "Not ever."

His words settle deep into my chest. I blink quickly, hoping to keep holding the tears back, but they're right there. Right on the edge.

"I won't leave you either, Kota," I promise. "Ever."

Kota leans over and puts his arms around my neck, squeezing me in an embrace that causes my tears to drop and mix in with the rain.

I cast the oar aside and hug him back, and search deep into my memory to try and find a moment even remotely like this—something to compare it to—but I can't.

It's the first time I've ever felt needed.

Chapter 25

The next few hours are a blur. Kota and I are both on high alert.

Every movement in the trees brings the immediate fear of another bobcat, and even when things seem still, the aching in my arm reminds me how real our situation is. We are lost, we are hurting, and everything, even the rain falling from the sky, seems more dangerous than before.

"I think I should be the one rowing, not you," Kota announces as he extends his hands to take the oar. "You need to rest."

"But you need rest too," I argue. "In fact, we should both be resting."

Physically, I hurt in almost every place I can think of, and mentally, I've had the same thought eating at my mind since Markell said it aloud.

What if The Hill isn't safe?

Or worse, what if my decision to find it puts us both in danger?

I look back at Kota still struggling to breathe in the damp, heavy air without coughing. If we stay here, if we keep wandering without a real plan, we won't last. Maybe The Hill is dangerous. But maybe it's not. It's the only plan we have.

I tighten the cloth around my arm, swallowing my fear.

"We need to rest," I say again, my voice steadier than I feel. "We just have to."

"Maybe we don't paddle, then," Kota suggests. "I can guide the canoe as it floats."

I'm reluctant to have Kota do anything after what he has been through, but if I don't get any rest, I won't be able to help anyone, including myself.

"Okay, you can steer the boat, but no paddling," I concede. "Save your energy."

I hand Kota the oar and sit on the floor of the canoe, leaning back into the seat to give my lower back some needed relief.

"Should we just keep going this way?" Kota asks, pointing to the small separation between the tree-tops. "It seems the easiest, and the current is pushing us there anyway."

"We need to get out of the forest to see where we are," I say to him. "I think that's our best bet."

"Got it," Kota confirms in a commanding voice. "You relax. I'll steer."

Over the next several hours, Kota does just that. It's the longest break I've had so far since leaving the city, and I sense my strength coming back as I go through a few cans of food and spend the time watching the forest for signs of anything potentially dangerous—or, better yet, lifesaving. Kota takes the occasional break to eat as well, but we don't talk much as he navigates the gaps between the trees.

Sometimes, it seems like we are about to break through. We'll emerge from a line of trees into an open area, maybe the size of a football field, only to see more trees surrounding the clearing, like a reverse oasis.

"Not again," Kota groans from the front. "I thought this was wide-open water coming up."

For the rest of the day, this is how it goes. Glimmers of hope, only to be dashed by more and more trees.

As night falls, it becomes clear we are not leaving the forest anytime soon.

"We should find a place to anchor the canoe for the night," I suggest as Kota skims the oar over the surface of the brown water. "Let's see if we can find some sort of cover."

Kota continues to navigate, weaving around the floating chunks of bark as we glide deeper into the dense forest. The darkness adds to the difficulty, and the path through twisted trunks rising from the dark water seems almost endless.

I tighten my grip on the sides of the canoe, pulse thrumming in my ears.

Each direction looks like the last. Every tree looks like the others. It's all the same.

"Um, I don't know which way to go," murmurs

Kota, his voice hoarse from the coughing. "I'm getting confused."

As I scan the water ahead to try and find an answer, I notice a collection of branches that doesn't seem natural. They aren't jutting out horizontally from the trunk like they do on the rest of the trees. Instead, they are all slanted at a 45-degree angle, and they seem to be tethered together.

"There!" I shout, sitting up to point out what I see to Kota. "Check out that tree over there!"

"Is that a fort or something?" he asks as he takes the flashlight out of his jacket to cut through the incoming dusk. "It seems man-made."

The closer we get, the more obvious the structure becomes. Not only are the branches tied together to form a roof but there seems to be a small platform too. Multiple cut logs have been fastened together, and although they are partially submerged, there is no denying their purpose. It's a dock!

I take out my flashlight and scan the area for any other signs of people, but all I can see is tree after tree after tree.

"Should I get us over there?" Kota asks, turning to me. "What do you think?"

"I think that if it gets us out of the rain, we should do it," I announce, pointing my flashlight at the rugged structure. "It's getting dark, and I can't imagine that anyone would try and go through the forest at night."

Kota nods and puts the oar back in the water, steering us closer to the fort. The canoe floats gently up onto the logs until we are underneath the protection of the branches. We tie it safely to one of them.

"This is pretty lucky," Kota declares as he puts the oar into the boat for the night. "It's actually dry in here too."

Dry is a loose term. Rain is dripping through the overlapping branches and needles, but at least the canoe won't flood with water throughout the night. I start to move Markell's bag out from under a steady stream of drops, but an object catches my eye from within the bag.

"No way," I say, pulling out a dark-green tarp. "I wish we would've dug deeper in this bag sooner."

The green tarp is much smaller than the last one we had, but it's large enough for us to partially cover the canoe and ourselves as we crunch in next to each other at the base of it.

"Aurora?" Kota says after a few minutes of silence. "Do you think there are other people like us out there?"

"What do you mean?" I ask. "In canoes?"

Kota pushes closer to me as we both try to get more comfortable.

"I just mean . . ." he begins, his voice trailing off. "I mean . . . do you think there are other *kids* out there, doing the same thing as us?"

I hadn't thought about that. Everyone we have

seen so far has been older, which is a strange thing to think about.

"There must be," I assure him. "And I bet we meet some when we get to The Hill."

"That's good," Kota says, the warmth from his breath brushing my face. "I bet they will love meeting you."

Even though Kota and I are still kids, I feel more like an adult as we lie here together, like I've suddenly traded my own thoughts for the kind with the weight that parents carry. I wrap my arms around him and hug him close as he turns his back to me, then squeeze tighter, hoping it will chase away the day's worries—both his and mine. For a moment, I imagine I can pour out all my fear and exhaustion, as if holding him is somehow holding us together.

We settle into the canoe, the forest curling in around us, as I try to prepare myself for tomorrow, whatever it may bring.

Chapter 26

I wake with a start.

For a moment, I forget where I am. Everything feels wrong. The air is heavy, and deep, whooshing sounds seem to come from all around, which disorients me even more.

"What is that sound?" Kota asks. The tarp above us flaps in the wind. "It's so loud!"

I reach to remove the protective cover of the tarp, but a gust of wind tries to rip it from my grasp. As I fight to wield it back into the canoe, Kota sits up and joins me. We take in what is happening.

It's a storm.

Water laps at the sides of the canoe as another rush of wind tears through the trees. Branches creak and snap, the sound sharp like gunfire, and I flinch. One of the branches crashes a few feet away, sending up a spray of icy cold water that splashes across my face.

"Don't let go!" I yell to Kota. We fight the wind together, yanking the tarp as it twists in the air.

Rain pounds everything in sight, a thousand tiny hammers drilling into the surface of the churning water. I blink hard and look up. The sky is nothing but swirling gray, the clouds churning like a massive whirlpool.

We pull the tarp over our heads just as a large gust of wind howls through the canopy of the forest, snapping branches and hurling them like spears. Another massive limb crashes into the water beyond the structure, while pine-needle bullets fly in all directions.

"Pull it down!" Kota yells. He ducks into the bottom of the canoe.

Instead of pulling it, however, I yank the edge of the tarp tightly around the outside of my face like a hood, and try to assess the situation as quickly as possible. The top of the tree next to us gives up completely and falls with a splintering crack as it crashes into the flood, sending a wave that picks the canoe up off the crude dock and slams it back down again.

"Hold on!" I yell to Kota as I try to join him, but my breath catches and the wind blasts me backward. I dive back down again, this time landing next to Kota, pulling the tarp as close to us as possible.

All around us is the sound of destruction: howling winds, churning water, and the constant snap and crash of trees breaking apart. The forest feels alive, like it's fighting the storm and losing, one piece at a time.

The battering of the canoe continues for hours while Kota and I cling to each other. There isn't a single break as the wind persists, ripping through the trees and preventing us from doing anything other than hope the storm will let up soon.

But it doesn't.

All night and into day, it rages on, plummeting more and more treetops into the water.

"What should we do?!" Kota yells as the tarp continues to ripple above our heads. "Should we try and leave?"

"We can't paddle through this!" I yell back as another large snap breaks through the wind. "We just need to outlast the storm!"

We hunker down closer to each other, and do the only thing we are able to do.

Wait.

It isn't until nightfall when the air around us becomes suspiciously still. We wait for a moment, anticipating another onslaught of wind, but it never comes. Finally, after a full day trying to outlast the storm, Kota and I are able to remove the tarp and take a look around.

The forest—or what's left of it—looks frail and weak. Trees are snapped in all directions, some leaning on each other for support while others have plunged into the water, their branches now shooting up toward the clear sky.

Clear.

"Wow," says Kota, stunned. He gazes upward. "I can't remember the last time I saw the moon."

"I can't either," I add as I scan the night sky. "I think it's a full moon too."

For the first time since it started raining over a month ago, there isn't a single cloud in the sky, and the rain has completely stopped. It's eerie how different it seems after listening to rainfall for so long.

"I can't believe our tree didn't fall," Kota says, looking across the swampy-looking forest. "I thought it would for sure."

"Same," I agree. "We got pretty lucky."

We both look up at our strong tree as the moonlight brightens the now-destroyed fort. The tied branches that covered us are mostly gone except for a few remaining wood poles that held them in place. And now that the canopy above us is gone, too, I can almost see the top of the tree.

"This tree is huge!" Kota points out, slapping the truck with his hand. "We should climb it, don't you think?"

"And why would we do that?" I ask.

"Because then we could see where to go!"

Kota's right. With a clear sky and a full moon above us, we might be able to see farther than we ever have before, and possibly a way out of the forest.

"It's worth a shot," I say as I remove the hood from around my face. "I'll go."

"No," Kota says firmly. "Your arm is hurt, remember? Plus, I'm smaller, so the branches are less likely to snap under me."

I look up to the top of the tree again to assess the risk, but Kota is already standing up and bracing himself against the tree.

"You've already taken a risk by getting the canoe," I point out. "This seems like something I should do, not you."

Kota frowns. "But if I go up there with the map and see some sort of landmark, then I might be able to navigate us to The Hill," he says.

I let out a deep sigh, because he is right. If I go up there, I may not know what I am looking at, and it could be a waste.

"Okay, fine. You can go. Just be careful," I warn as I steady the canoe. "Take each step slowly."

Kota doesn't respond. He grabs the first visible branch and pulls himself effortlessly up into the tree.

"Careful," I warn again, though I doubt Kota can hear me. He's too focused. Still, one wrong move, one slippery branch, and he'll fall. My stomach knots as I clutch the edge of the canoe, torn between wanting to call him down and knowing we need this. I hold my breath, silently begging the tree to hold steady as Kota climbs higher and higher until he is out of sight.

"I'm almost to the top!" Kota shouts from above.

"Can you see anything yet?" I yell, wishing I was up there too. "How far can you see?"

"I think I see the edge of the forest!" he declares. "And I see . . ."

There is a long, drawn-out pause before I hear Kota again.

"There's something in the forest!" he yells. "It's a fire or light or something!"

With everything completely saturated from the storm, the likelihood of a fire starting seems impossible. Still, I scan the flooded forest, my eyes darting over the water and the broken remains of trees jutting out like splintered bones. Everything is gray and light blue as the moonlight blankets the storm-ravaged forest, but then—something.

A flicker.

I freeze, struggling to see as droplets slip off the branches above.

There, in the distance, a pinprick of orange light wavers, bobbing up and down like it's alive. A flame?

My brain struggles to catch up.

The light doesn't grow or shrink, but it is moving closer.

People! It must be people!

"Kota!" I gasp in a strangled whisper that's loud enough to rip through the stillness. "Get down, now!"

"What?" Kota's voice shatters the silence, too loud, too careless. "Should I come down?"

"Shh! Yesss! *Now!*" I hiss, urgency choking the words. "Someone's coming!"

The crack of snapping branches reaches my ears. He's moving, but too slowly.

"Hurry!" I call again, heart hammering in my chest. I turn toward the creeping glow of the flame. "We need to go! *Now!*"

But Kota's not moving fast enough. If he takes as long as he did to climb up, the light—and whoever's bringing it—will get here first.

What do I do? What do I do?!

Panic claws at my throat, almost suffocating me. I close my eyes for a second. A decision has to be made. Now.

If I climb up after him, the canoe could be stolen. If I stay, we'll both be caught. But if I leave . . . if I leave, maybe—just maybe—he can stay quiet, stay still, and whoever's coming will pass us by, never knowing we were here.

"Kota, go back up!" I shout, desperation bleeding into my voice. I no longer care how loud we're being. "I'll move the canoe. Just don't move, okay? Don't move!"

"No, don't leave me!" his voice cracks, the sound of pure fear ripping through the air. "I don't want to be alone!"

"Stay still! Stay quiet!" I bark. With no time for any more directions, I grab the oar and push the canoe off the dock.

I'll stay close, close enough.

I paddle the canoe in the opposite direction of

the incoming light until I see a tall collection of fallen branches tangled in the water, about fifty yards away.

Perfect. Hidden from view, with a clear sightline to the tree.

I quickly maneuver the canoe to the backside of the stacked trees, hugging them close so not a single part of the canoe can be seen. As soon as I'm fully on the other side, I hear a deep voice.

"Wow," the voice begins. "The storm really tore the place apart."

I slowly peek my head over the pile of floating branches to get a glimpse. The moonlight is just bright enough to outline the shadow of a man.

"Put some more oil on that torch," another voice commands. "I can barely see a thing out here."

In an instant, the small light in the distance leaps and swells into a brilliant flare. The darkness is banished as the light stretches farther, flickering boldly against the dark water and revealing the source of the voices.

It's two people, a man and woman. They are both standing in a small craft not much larger than our canoe.

"How far are we supposed to go?" the woman asks, holding the torch higher into the air.

"They said until we reach the far dock, then come back to report," the man says, pointing directly at the fort Kota and I were just on. "I'm surprised we even found it after the damage the storm caused."

A branch snaps above them.

Come on, Kota. You can do this. Don't move!

The man spins and grabs the torch from the woman, holding it high into the air as he looks up toward the tree.

Hold still, Kota!

Another snapping sound, this time louder than the last.

"Up there!" the man says. "Do you see that?"

"Probably an animal," the woman says, uncaring. "Lucky to be alive after that storm."

The man doesn't flinch. He keeps his torch and eyes upward.

I hold my breath, hoping Kota is doing the same.

The man reaches behind him and digs into the lining of his pants before bringing his arm forward, revealing a small pistol.

"I see you!" the man growls, raising his weapon to align with the torch. "Get down here, or I'll shoot!"

The woman steps beside him, her voice sharp and cutting. "Someone's up there?"

"Don't tempt me!" the man snarls again toward the tree, his knuckles bulging around the grip of the gun. "It wouldn't be the first time I've shot someone."

He's bluffing. He has to be bluffing!

"Please don't!" Kota begs, his voice cracking through the silence. "I'm just a kid! Don't shoot!"

No, Kota! No!

The man's torchlight flickers as Kota descends.

Branches snap under his weight, loud and echoing in the night air. The man's weapon tracks him with eerie precision, its muzzle unwavering, until Kota's shoes thud softly against the dock.

"Who else is with you?" the man barks, his voice a whip of anger as he thrusts the gun closer, only inches from Kota's face.

"No one!" Kota blurts, squeezing his eyes shut and turning his cheek away. "I swear! I'm alone!"

"We'll see about that," the man spits. He thrusts the torch into the woman's hands before twisting back around, faster than Kota can react.

In one brutal motion, he snatches Kota by the collar, yanks him forward as though he weighs nothing, and presses the barrel into Kota's ribs.

"You listen to me, boy," he snarls. "You're going to answer every question I ask, or I'll use this and leave you out here for the animals. Do you understand?"

Kota trembles, his breath hitching, because he doesn't know the truth, like I do.

Guns can't shoot anymore.

I lower my hand until I can feel the metal handle of my hatchet and grip it with everything I have.

I'm coming, Kota.

*And nothing—*nothing*—is going to stop me this time.*

Chapter 27

There isn't another moment to spare.

I can see a clear path to Kota, but I can't risk being seen on the water. Even though the fallen branches float in a jagged formation, their splintered ends are tethered together by moss and decay, creating a series of half-sunken bridges jutting out in all directions.

If I'm quiet enough—if I'm stealthy—I can cross them and get close.

Close enough to attack.

I crouch low as I step out of the canoe onto the nearest tree. It shifts under my weight, bobbing sluggishly. Quickly, I tug the stern of the canoe onto the bark to keep it from drifting away. It's not secure, far from it, but it will have to do.

I get down on my hands and knees to crawl, but the tree is slick. Each time I move, the bark peels away to reveal a spongy layer of rot that fills my nose with a composting stench. I have to press my body flat to avoid sliding off completely. Each pull along the tree is a balancing act, the damp moss smearing my arms and the tip of my nose. But again, I slide my body forward.

Just ahead, the man's sharp voice rips through the swampy, flooded forest.

"Where did you come from?!" he barks. "How did you get here?!"

Kota's voice trembles. "The city. I was in an apartment, and I—"

His sentence trails off as I pull myself to the next pile of broken trees. Each movement feels like I'm hanging on a thread; the slightest shift could rotate everything beneath me, plunging me into the dark, cold water. It's taking all of my energy to squeeze and stabilize myself with every pull.

I turn my head to the side to catch my breath, and I grab my hatchet from its sheath. The man continues to press Kota.

"No way you came here on your own. You must have a party with you!" he accuses. "Where are they?! How many are there?!"

I need to get closer! Keep pulling. Keep moving!

"I promise you!" Kota shouts back, pleading. "I'm all alone!"

My muscles burn as I drag myself across another log, and with each inch closer, the tension in my chest tightens like a coiled spring. I'm just near enough now to see Kota's face—wide-eyed and pale—as the hatchet rests in my grip.

I swallow hard, steadying my breath. The man

doesn't see me yet, but one wrong move, one loud creak or splash, and it's over.

I have to act before it's too late.

"I don't believe him," the woman says as I slide onto the next log. "But I also don't think he is going to tell us anything here. Let's take him back."

I pause.

Take him back? Back where?!

Kota's eyes flicker between the man and the woman, who are now looking at each other underneath the light of the torch.

"Plus," the woman continues, "we can just have Irene question him. She'll get the info out. She always does."

"Maybe," he considers. "But if *we* come back with information and save Irene the time, think about the recognition we'll get! Might be enough to boost us up to the next rationing level."

"More food . . ." the woman remarks, staring at Kota. "All right, let's see what we can get out of him, then."

The man pushes Kota against the trunk of the large tree.

There isn't any more time! I have to do it now!

With a sharp inhale, I rise to one knee, steadying myself on the unstable collection of bark and splintered trees. My arm draws back, the motion almost instinctive. The frame of the hatchet feels alive, its potential humming in the palm of my hand, as my focus narrows on the man, just above where his arm flexes as he reaches toward Kota.

Left foot forward. Steady . . .

"Boy, you better tell me something I want to hear now," he continues, "or I'm going to make the next few minutes miserable for you."

There's no fear this time. Just strength. Quiet, powerful strength.

Wait for it . . . wait for it . . .

Kota pulls away as the man leans closer, his shadow swallowing Kota's small, trembling frame.

Now!

I let the hatchet fly.

It spins through the air, end over end, the sharp head gleaming faintly in the moonlight.

Time seems to slow as it arcs toward the target, cutting through the air with a whistling hum.

Then, with a sickening *THUNK*, it embeds itself into the man's shoulder.

His scream rips through the trees as the force of the blow spins him sideways. He stumbles, arms flailing, and crashes into the edge of the floating dock as his gun topples into the water.

"*Aiken!*" the woman bellows before spinning around to see where the attack came from.

Kota springs forward, shoving the woman and sending her flailing into the murky water.

I don't waste the moment and quickly traverse the next few trees. Each step on the slick, unstable debris is a blur, my focus locked on Kota and the man crumpled on the dock.

"That way!" I shout, pointing back the way I came from. "Run!"

Kota doesn't need to be told twice.

He frantically scrambles past me onto the floating logs, but behind him, the man stirs, his body writhing in pain. He's face down with the hatchet still embedded deep in his shoulder. Its handle juts out like a cruel lever.

A growl escapes his throat as he starts to push himself up from the dock.

No!

Without thinking, I lunge forward and rip the hatchet free. The man lets out another piercing scream, his body convulsing with pain.

I spin on my heel and take off after Kota, my feet sloppily pounding against the unsteady terrain as I pass the woman struggling to pull herself out of the water and onto a nearby tree. The flame of the torch is gone, so the scene has become a series of shadows, the moon creating just enough light to forge ahead.

"Kota!" I yell as I race to catch up. "Don't stop!"

There's no time to see if anyone is following.

All that matters is getting back to the canoe.

Shouting erupts behind us as our canoe comes into view, bobbing unsteadily against the edge of the floating trees. Kota gets in first and pushes off. I jump in next to him. I grab the oar and shove it into the water, paddling urgently while the shouting continues.

"Let's go!" I bark.

The water churns with each plunge of the oar, and the gash in my arm screams as the canoe jerks forward.

Kota kneels at the front, shoving aside the debris in front of us.

"Faster!" Kota yells, his voice trembling. "Go, go, go!"

I paddle harder, slamming the oar into the water with wild, desperate strokes. The canoe jerks and grinds over the submerged timber and jagged logs scraping against the hull as my heart pounds while I paddle, but the storm has turned the forest into a maze. Every direction is blocked by a tangle of broken trees and floating wreckage, each waterway clogged with obstacles that seem to multiply with every frantic push forward.

Behind us, the shouting morphs into a howl of frustration, but I don't look back. The oar almost slips out of my hands, slick with water and sweat, as the canoe grates against another pile of debris.

"We're not moving fast enough!" I gasp.

The storm has turned the swamp into a trap, but there's no going back now.

It's forward or nothing.

We suddenly hit an open path, a clear vein of water splitting through the trees. The next push from the oar spits us forward, and we gain speed with each rhythmic stroke.

"Faster!" Kota begs. "Faster!"

My eyes squeeze shut as I dig deep for every morsel of energy in my body. I push and pull the oar as fast and hard as I can.

"Look out!" Kota yells.

The canoe jolts abruptly as it slams into something solid. The force throws me sideways, and my chest hits the edge of the boat, sending the oar out of my hands and into the water as the canoe tilts dangerously to one side.

Kota pushes frantically against the object blocking the canoe with no success.

"We're stuck!" he yells, his voice cracking with panic. "I can't move it!"

My lungs burn as I finally gasp in a breath, just in time to see something I hoped I'd never see again.

A small flame flickers to life in front of us, illuminating the water with a haunting yellow glow.

Then another ignites to our left.

A third blazes to life on our right.

Kota freezes. I wrap one arm around him protectively, pulling him close. My other hand grips the hatchet tightly, ready for whatever comes next.

The firelight bounces across the dark water, casting eerie, shifting shadows.

The swamp erupts with light as two more torches blaze to life, revealing a sprawling network of interconnected docks. The massive structure floats in front of us, its planks warped, rotted, and broken, but sturdy enough to hold what steps forward.

A group of figures emerges from the shadows, their faces obscured by the flickering light. Some hold weapons: rusted machetes, makeshift clubs, and knives that glint in the firelight.

One man steps closer, his torch illuminating his narrow eyes as he takes in the hatchet clenched in my hand.

"Drop the axe, kid," he says, low and menacing. "You're surrounded."

Two women step forward, too, grabbing the canoe and yanking it fully onto the dock. Before I can make a move, two men grab my shoulders. One pries the hatchet from my hand, and then it clangs on the canoe floor.

"Let me go!" Kota yells as he is plucked from his seat by another man.

"Don't let either of them go," a voice growls from the shadows of the group. "The taller one is stronger than she looks."

That sends a chill down my spine. My head snaps toward the voice, and my stomach twists.

It's him—Aiken, the injured man.

He's standing hunched over, one hand clutching a bloodstained piece of fabric pressed against his shoulder. His face is pale but twisted, with a hateful fury that makes my blood run cold.

"Once we get what we need from you," he says, voice dripping with vengeance, "you better believe I'll pay you back for this."

I try to plant my feet, but it's useless. The two men gripping my arms drag me forward, my boots scraping and bouncing against the uneven planks of the dock.

Every jolt sends a sharp ache up my legs, but I can't stop staring at Aiken, his menacing smirk deepening the closer I get.

"Tie them both up," he commands, his voice gaining strength despite the strain in his body. Then he gestures across the dock with a sharp jab. "Put them in the main boat, and grab their supplies too. I don't want any more surprises tonight."

"Got it," the man to my right replies as his grip tightens around my arm, sending pulses of pain through my body. "And where to next? Another checkpoint?"

"No," Aiken says. He turns slowly and walks down the uneven dock. The boards snap and creak, each sound amplified in the silence.

He stops to grab a torch resting in a slot of a large upright beam, then glances back over his shoulder with a cold smile.

"We're headed back to The Hill."

Chapter 28

Kota's eyes meet mine as two of Aiken's men forcefully guide us down the dock until we approach a boat, one that is much larger than anything I've seen since leaving the mansion. But like everything else has become since the rain came, the boat is clearly damaged. Its hull is so scarred and dented it seems like it should be sunken at the bottom of the ocean instead of floating in front of us.

"Get in," the man orders.

My feet stay planted on the dock as I try to think of a plan, any plan, that will keep Kota and me from going with them.

"Tie her up," Aiken orders, tossing the man a coil of rope. "And the boy too."

I'm quickly spun around, and the rope is lassoed around each of my wrists, its wiry barbs digging into my skin. I watch as the same is done to Kota while his panicked eyes dart between the men and me. He struggles for a moment, thrashing against their hold, but it only makes them pull the rope tighter.

"Stop squirming!" one of the men barks, shoving Kota forward so hard he stumbles and nearly falls over.

"Kota!" I call out, but before I can say anything more, a sharp yank on my own bindings forces me forward.

"We don't have all night," Aiken snaps, his voice a mix of pain and impatience. He gestures toward the looming boat while its shadowy, ghostly outline rocks gently in the dark water. "Get them on board, and make it quick."

The men hauling us don't hesitate. Kota glances back at me, but there's nothing I can do to reassure him as we're both shoved aboard the ominously creaking boat.

"Put 'em up front," Aiken says as he walks behind us, taking the position behind the steering wheel. "We're headed back to The Hill tonight."

"In the dark?" the woman asks. "Isn't that too risky? We won't be able to see any of the holes in the water."

"Shui gui," Kota mumbles sadly from the front. "It's the shui gui."

Aiken ignores Kota and continues.

"I'm more concerned about these two," he says, gesturing to Kota and me as a man pushes us to the front of the boat. "I think they're hiding something from us. If they're part of a larger group, then Irene needs to know. *Tonight.*"

Irene. That's the second time he's mentioned that name. Who is Irene?

"Fine," the woman says, clearly irritated. "But if we lose another boat to the holes, that's on you, and you can explain it to Irene."

Aiken scoffs at her as more of the crew begin to tether their smaller canoes, including ours, to the side of the larger boat.

"Ready," a man declares from one of them, then covers the flame of his torch with a cap.

The rest of the crew extinguish their torches as well, leaving just one last flicker of light remaining at Aiken's side, casting enough of a glow to illuminate our boat and the others tied to it.

Kota and I sit with our backs to the bow, our eyes fixed on Aiken as the boat's motor hums to life and we move forward.

I swallow against the dryness in my throat.

Niko and Jada . . . will they be there, or are they somewhere else, searching for me? Or worse, are they even alive?

"Are we really going to The Hill?" Kota whispers.

"I think so," I whisper back, my eyes still locked on Aiken. "Are you hurt at all?"

"No," Kota assures me. "I'm just scared."

I am too. But for Kota, I need to try to be something else.

"It will be okay," I say, turning my body to allow his to snuggle into me. "We just need to wait for an opportunity."

Kota buries his face into my chest as the boat pushes forward, dragging the other tethered vessels with it.

The path ahead is clearer, but not by much, as the side canoes occasionally scrape up against floating trees and rotten wood. Each jolt of the craft spooks the crew, who diligently watch over the sides.

I can only assume they are watching for Dark Pools, or as they called them, *holes.*

With the torch flickering at the center of the boat and the moonlight spilling across the clear sky, the changes in scenery are impossible to miss. Minute by minute, hour by hour, the trees diminish in number, but the ones that remain seem to be growing over time. The forest trees that once only stuck out four or five feet above the water now rise to double that height, creating the illusion that either the water is lowering or we're drifting uphill.

Kota notices the same thing.

"Aurora, I think the elevation is changing beneath us," he says, breaking the silence and gesturing with his head to a nearby tree. "I think we might be getting closer to The Hill."

"I agree," I whisper back as I scan the horizon. "If that's the case, we need to have a plan."

"A plan? What plan do you—"

Kota pauses as a crew member stands up. For a second, I think he may have heard us, but instead the man takes a long stretch with his hands high in the air before sitting back down, and Kota resumes his thought.

"What plan do you have in mind?" he asks.

"Not a good one," I admit. "But I want to make sure of two things: I want to try to stay together if we can, and I want to make sure we have the same story."

Another crew member glances in our direction. I do a fake yawn, then push my face down next to Kota's like I'm sleeping.

"Close your eyes tight, and don't talk," I whisper into his ear. "I am going to tell you the things I want you to remember to say when we are questioned."

I keep my eyes closed and tell Kota the lie I want him to remember.

"We are brother and sister. We lived in an apartment in the city with our father, Markell. The city burned down, and we escaped on a canoe to the forest. We are with no one else."

End of story.

I am not sure why I decided to change our past. Maybe acting like a family will keep us together, if we are lucky.

Because right now, we are not lucky at all.

I continue to repeat the story to Kota until I am interrupted by an announcement.

"There!" a crew member says. "I see the beacon."

Kota sits up and turns around to face the front of the boat, and I do the same. There is a bright light ahead, but it's not a flame. Instead, a beam shoots across the water, scanning in all directions until it pauses on our boat, making it almost impossible for me to see forward.

"Welcome to The Hill," Aiken says to no one in particular. "The paradise above the water."

A few crew members chuckle as they untie the ropes binding the canoes together. Once they are disconnected, they float away a few at a time, and when the last canoe is finally untethered, our boat picks up speed, heading straight into the bright light ahead. The intensity of it makes the little I could see around us vanish and obscures any view of the upcoming surroundings as the water sloshes against the battered hull of the boat.

"We're going to be okay," I assure Kota, and I squeeze his bound hands with mine. "We're in this together."

Kota squeezes back as the engine is cut off and the boat dramatically slows down. The change of speed almost knocks Kota and me from our seats to the ground as our backs slam up against the bow of the boat. I still can't see anything ahead of us other than a blur of light, but I can hear the flurry of motion around us:

The footsteps clattering on planks.

The waves lapping against objects around us.

And voices.

Many, many voices.

Aiken steps onto the dock with ease, his eyes

straining to focus against the brightness but clearly more familiar than I am with what's ahead. He doesn't seem as affected by the overwhelming light as the rest of us.

"The Hill," he says, his voice full of cold sarcasm. "The place that's supposed to save us all. Well, some of us, at least."

The bright light abruptly shuts off, and I have to blink multiple times for my eyes to adjust. When I can finally focus them, what is in front of me seems unreal.

The dock stretches forward into what looks like a desolate, half-constructed town. Large, unfinished structures tower around us, casting long shadows. Switchback roads lead upward, connecting a series of large tunnel entrances, some of which seem recently constructed while others are barricaded with large metal doors encased in a metallic dome.

"What is this place?" Kota asks, his voice laced with disbelief.

Aiken seems entertained by Kota's trance.

"Not bad, right?" he says, gesturing for us to step out of the boat. "That's what planning will do, unlike all the sunken idiots in the world."

"So much for being labeled as the 'crazy people,' huh?" the woman sneers as she pushes Kota and me down the dock behind Aiken. "I enjoyed watching them all grovel when they realized how helpless they were, once the world stopped being what they knew."

Aiken lets out a deep, hearty laugh.

"Absolutely. Rule number one seemed to work out pretty good for us, didn't it?"

Rule number one?!

As in Niko's rule?

"Well, it did help to find like-minded people," the woman adds, joining in Aiken's laughter. "And to think, after all these years of waiting and prepping . . ."

Prepping?!

". . . we would finally get a chance to be on top and make some decisions. But we have Irene to thank for that."

The woman turns to the rest of the crew.

"Hey! How about a cheer for Irene, huh?!" she calls. "The one who made this all possible. For Irene!"

The group, including Aiken, all put their fists in the air.

"Irene!"

"One more time!"

"Irene!"

"Stand with The Hill!" Aiken interjects, yelling even louder.

"Or do not stand at all!" the crew finishes, erupting in cheers that echo between the buildings and the mountainside.

The group pivots in unison, moving us farther down the dock toward the makeshift city.

My mind races.

The Hill—the place I hoped all along would be a sanctuary, a place of hope—doesn't feel anything like that.

In fact, it feels like the exact opposite.

But there's no choice to be made right now.

We are here. We have arrived at The Hill.

Chapter 29

Aiken and his crew move us down the dock and onto dry land. The structures are not like any sort of buildings I've seen before. Instead of consisting of corners and rectangles, they are circular, with rounded tops and curved sides, like bubbles coming out of the ground. They overlap each other, too, as if some are expanding off the others.

"Come on! Stop dragging your feet!" Aiken bellows as another forceful shove hits me in the back. "Get walking!"

I put my head back down and continue to walk forward as I stare at the ground beneath me. After being surrounded by water for so long, seeing grass is a strange sight. It's like stepping into a once-forgotten memory, familiar and distant at the same time.

"This way," Aiken instructs, interrupting my thoughts. He tugs at my arm, pulling me off the grass and onto a rocky gravel path that heads up the small mountainside. It's so steep that within just a few steps I am already breathing heavily.

I worry for Kota, who is behind me in line somewhere. I can't turn around to check on him for risk of tripping over my own feet and falling, so I continue forward, hoping that somehow, an opportunity to escape will present itself.

We walk uphill for a few more minutes until the path plateaus and we find ourselves standing in front of a smaller dome structure. It has a single solid door in the front, and on either side are small circular lights that jut out from beneath the building, casting shadows from the framing that surrounds the giant window at the top.

"Bring the other one up!" Aiken commands sharply, not bothering to glance back as he strides toward the door. A rough shove sends Kota stumbling into me, and we both have to adjust until we are standing shoulder to shoulder.

We exchange a brief, uneasy glance before turning our attention to Aiken.

He reaches for the heavy door and sends out a forceful knock that echoes through the still air. Then, without a word, he steps back, and the rest of the men straighten their stances. The tone of the group is charged with an unspoken tension as we wait for whatever comes next.

BANG! The door erupts with the metallic clatter of latches opening.

A woman steps into view, and I'm immediately struck by her imposing presence. She stands taller than Aiken—not by much, but enough to make it clear she commands the space. Her broad shoulders carry authority, emphasized by the strands of dark, unruly hair that fall over them. Her forearms are corded with muscles that flex slightly as she shoves her thumbs into her belt loops.

Every inch of her seems to radiate with power.

"Aiken," the woman says, low and haunting, "back from patrol so soon?"

"Yes," Aiken replies. His voice is tight, almost hesitant, as he looks to Kota and me. "We didn't want to come back early, but we have a good reason, Irene."

Irene!

My stomach twists.

"I should hope so," Irene says, leaning casually against the doorframe, her piercing gaze locked on Aiken. "Because you *broke* a rule."

Her words settle over the group like a heavy fog. Some of the men shift uneasily, like their confidence is wilting under her presence.

"I promise you," Aiken says, "we *had* to come back early. We found something."

Irene doesn't even glance in our direction, her focus still on Aiken, her expression unmoving.

"It was the *rules* that saved us, remember?" she says. Then she pushes off the doorframe and strides forward until she's mere inches from Aiken. "If we *break* the rules, we endanger the lives of everyone here. Is that what we want?"

Aiken falters, his mouth opening and closing as if searching for an answer.

Irene leans in closer, her face brushing past his until her lips hover near his ear, her voice dropping to a menacing whisper.

"Is it?" she asks. "Is that what we want, Aiken?"

"No," he answers. "That's not what we want."

Irene smiles and addresses the group.

"It was the rules that saved us!" she declares, her voice carrying a firm intensity as her eyes sweep across each face. "And it is the rules that will *continue* to save us!"

The silence that follows is deafening. She turns back to Aiken.

"Now," she says coolly, "what was so important that you had to break a rule?"

Aiken swallows and gestures toward us.

"We found these two by one of the lookouts. I think they're part of a larger network, but they won't tell me anything."

Irene's eyes flicker in our direction. For the first time, I feel the full grasp of her attention. It makes me feel small but visible, like a bug about to be crushed by a foot.

"They shouldn't tell you anything," Irene says, almost proud as she scans my face with her eyes. "They must be smart, or at the very least, loyal."

"The girl is dangerous too," the woman from the back of the group warns. "She almost escaped."

Irene begins to walk closer to me, but she stops short and looks back at Aiken.

"Looks like she got the better of you," she says, nodding toward Aiken's bandaged shoulder. I can tell her voice is calm, but there's no mistaking the edge beneath it. "Go down to the barracks and get stitched up."

"Irene, with all due respect," Aiken says, "I'd like to stay and—"

"No," Irene snaps as she shoves her hand into her pocket. She digs for a moment and then tosses a small rectangular object at Aiken. "You and the crew, get some extra food and rest. We'll talk later."

Her words might seem kind, but the undertone carries something heavier.

Aiken catches the object with a resigned expression, and his shoulders sag as he pockets it.

"Yes, Irene," he mutters.

Without another word, he turns and walks down the hillside, the rest of the crew following in silence. Their boots crunch softly against the gravel path as the sound fades with each step.

Just like that, Kota and I are left with Irene.

"I am going to cut your hands free," she announces as she removes a small knife from her back pocket. "It would be wise of you to not run away. There are consequences here for misbehavior."

She puts her hand on Kota's shoulder and spins him around to face me.

His eyes catch mine, wide open and screaming like he wants to bolt.

I catch his gaze and shake my head subtly.

Not now! Just stay calm.

This isn't the time, and I don't have a plan. For now, all we can do is hold our ground and hope for a better opportunity.

The rope on Kota's wrist snaps, and he rubs the soreness from his skin as Irene walks behind me. She looms over me as she saws through my bindings. Irene could easily take me out if she wanted to, and based on how the group reacted to her, they must have a reason to believe she can take them at any moment.

They kept us around this long, though. They must need us for a reason, at least for now.

The cord breaks, and Irene walks back toward the front door.

"Let's go inside," she says calmly, then pushes the door open. "We have a lot to discuss."

Chapter 30

Irene leads us into the building. From the outside, it seemed like a cold, unwelcoming dome, but the interior surprises me. It's compact yet strangely cozy, even though the place is dimly lit.

The entire home is visible from where we are standing because it is as circular inside as it is outside. There is a bed at the back, which has large wooden cabinets on either side. To the right is a fireplace and stove, both sculpted from a pale clay that seams the two together, just like the structures I saw when we first arrived.

The heart of the room is less organized, though. At the center is a sturdy table, surrounded by a few mismatched chairs. Scattered across its surface are maps and a radio that look as if they've seen frequent, urgent use.

The entire place feels lived-in but also tense, like every item here has an important role I don't understand.

"Sit down," Irene directs. She moves toward

a kettle that is whistling quietly on the stove. "I'm going to get us something to drink."

Kota and I settle into our seats at the table as Irene tilts the kettle, pouring steaming liquid into three rough clay mugs that match the fireplace and stove. She then grabs a small jar of powder, sprinkling its contents into each mug without any measurement. Before stirring any of them, she scoops all three mugs into her hands and strides over, setting one in front of each of us. The steam curls lazily upward, and its warmth drifts across the table, filling the air between us.

Irene puts her nose above her mug as she sits down and takes a big inhale.

"Ah, that's much better," she says before taking a small sip. "Now, let's hear what you have to say."

I look at Kota, who is already drinking despite the heat I can feel coming off my own mug. I take a small sip and am hit with an intense peppermint flavor, which opens my sinuses and makes me sniffle.

"Powerful, right?" Irene says, taking another sip. "I only took what I needed when the rain came, but this is something I felt I needed to have for special days, and today is a special day."

"Why is that?" I ask. I'm still looking at Kota to make sure he is okay.

"Two reasons." Irene motions toward the window. "One, it's been twenty-four hours without rain. That's the longest stretch of time we've had so far."

"And the other?" I ask hesitantly.

"Your arrival," Irene says. She stacks the maps into a pile. "You're the first kids *ever* on The Hill."

The announcement makes Kota stop mid-sip.

"Shocked?" Irene asks while pushing the pile of maps to the side. "You shouldn't be. Not everyone who sets out to reach The Hill makes it, and that includes the people who knew about it first. In any case, you made it here," she says, her tone changing sharply to accusatory. "Which begs the question: How did two kids know about The Hill?"

"We didn't know," I lie. "We thought—"

"I don't want to hear from you yet," interrupts Irene. She gazes at Kota. "I want to hear from *you*. What is your name?"

Kota looks at me like there's been a mistake.

"Um, my name is Kota," he says.

"Nice to meet you, Kota. I'm Irene—but you probably figured that out already," she says, leaning back in her chair with a calculating smile. "I need you to tell me the truth, Kota. I need you to tell me the truth so we can all be safe. And that is what I want the most right now, to keep everyone here safe."

Kota twists in my direction, but Irene stops him.

"Don't look at her, look at me," she commands, almost gently. "How did you know about The Hill?"

The question hangs in the air like a trap. I don't know how to answer, and worse, I don't know how Kota should respond.

"We heard about The Hill from the signs," Kota begins. "We saw some as we left the city."

"Oh, you're from the city," Irene says, eyes narrowing. "There are a lot of people in the city. You must be part of a large group, then, huh?"

"No, it's just Aurora and me."

Don't say too much, Kota! Less is better.

"Come now," Irene says, her voice swinging into a chuckle as she looks at the two of us. "You expect me to believe two kids came from the city and made it all the way here without anyone else? Past the thieves? Past the dangers of the water?!"

"The only reason we're here is because those men brought us," I add quickly, trying to bolster Kota's lie and get him out of the spotlight before he slips up. "We would've died out there in the forest. We weren't trying to get to this place. We didn't even know where it was."

Irene tilts her head slightly, her expression unreadable.

"Maybe," she replies, her voice low and measured. "Or maybe you *were* on your way here, purposefully. The forest is the only way here, and you were pretty far in."

Kota and I stay quiet.

"You know what I think?" Irene continues. "I think you are part of a larger group. A group looking for a place to take refuge . . . or a place to take for themselves. The Hill is not for anyone else but the ones who are already here. The ones who helped plan for it."

Her words hang in the air like a blade poised to drop. Kota and I exchange a fleeting glance but stay silent. Irene doesn't blink as her stare eats away at me, hoping for something to crack.

"Well, you'll have plenty of time to try to remember all the details while you rest," she announces as she takes a covered walkie-talkie from her hip. "Irene to Shift One, are you there?"

Static. Then there's a voice.

"Shift One, copy. What do you need?"

"I need you to escort two people to the Hold Building right now. And hurry up; we don't need an incident like last time."

The voice cuts in and out a few times before coming through clearly.

"Yes, Irene, on my way."

Irene clicks the walkie-talkie off and places it next to the maps.

"Aurora and Kota," Irene almost hums as she stands, "I wonder what tomorrow will bring you."

Kota and I sit in uneasy silence as Irene picks up the pile of maps and moves them to a small counter by the bed. One by one she folds and unfolds them again, with the crinkle of paper the only sound filling the room.

I want to ask her so many questions—about the maps, this place, her intentions—but the atmosphere of the situation is squeezing me like a vise. Every instinct is telling me to stay quiet. The tension feels like a thread pulled too tight, with one wrong word or move enough to snap it.

A knock echoes through the room, and as Irene moves from her table, her gaze flicks to us for just a second. Her face is unreadable, but her movements are precise as she steps away from the maps and heads toward door. She undoes the latches slowly, and the door creaks open just a sliver. She leans into the gap, whispering to whoever is on the other side.

I can't make out the words, but the tone in Irene's voice is serious. Then, after a moment that stretches too long, she pulls the door wider, and someone steps inside into the light.

My eyes are drawn to the man entering the room, and for a moment, everything else fades—the maps on the counter, the strength in Irene's posture, the smell of peppermint in front of me.

There is a familiarity about him I can't ignore: the shape of his shoulders, the way he carries himself as he walks in. The way his hair sticks to his forehead . . .

My brain pieces it all together, one detail at a time, until I fully recognize him.

Niko.

Chapter 31

Niko's eyes lock onto mine, his expression a mirror of the panic I'm sure is plastered across my own face. His gaze darts from me to Irene, and his lips clamp shut like he's physically restraining himself from saying something. He trails Irene up to the table with stiff, mechanical steps, his nervousness palpable even from across the room.

"Kids, you'll be seeing me at some point tomorrow," Irene says. "Unless you have anything else you've decided to share before then?"

Out of Irene's line of sight, Niko's hand twitches at his side before he raises it slowly, pressing one finger firmly against his lips as his panicked stare holds on to mine. The silent warning both terrifies and confuses me.

Why is he doing that?

Why shouldn't I say anything?

I hesitate, then give the smallest shake of my head to Irene, which causes her to laugh.

"You are bold, I'll give you that," she says while

returning to the door and gesturing outside. "We'll try to talk more tomorrow."

Niko nods to Irene and then turns around as Kota and I stand up and follow him out into the night.

As soon as Irene shuts the door behind us, Niko clicks on a flashlight and quickly walks in the direction we came.

Does he expect me to follow him without any explanation or reasoning? How can he just move on without acknowledging what he put me through?!

I follow closely as I decide what I want to say to him first, but he soon stops at a split in the path. He takes one look around, scans the glowing buildings around us, then grabs my upper arm and pulls me close as we walk quickly down the gravel path.

"Don't. Say. Anything," he murmurs, while loosening the grip on my shoulder. "Wait until we get inside."

If I didn't know Niko, I would've already grabbed Kota and run in the opposite direction. We could easily make our way back down to the boats, even without the flashlight.

But I do know Niko. Not well, but well enough to know part of me still wants to trust him, even though nothing about the situation makes sense.

You better have an explanation, Niko. And it better be a good one.

Niko clicks off his flashlight and then leads us down a winding path, but not the same one we came from earlier. This route snakes through rows of structures eerily similar to Irene's—smaller but unmistakably cut from the same design. Each building has an identical front door, the same lighting, and the same windows that now seem like empty, watchful eyes as we weave through the makeshift neighborhood.

Who built all of this? Is this an actual town?

As we move deeper, the repetition of buildings continues. Every time I expect the path to change, to curve toward something different, we're greeted by another line of domed structures that stretches endlessly into the distance, the curved roofs glowing faintly under the sparse lights, creating the illusion of an infinite, uniform beehive. The farther we go, the less it feels like we're walking through a community and more like we're threading through a mirrored maze.

Finally, after what feels like an eternity of walking, the landscape shifts. Jutting out from the underside of the hill is a massive rectangular structure. Thick diagonal beams brace it against the hill's slope, giving it an almost skeleton-like appearance.

"What is that place?" Kota asks as we continue forward. "Is it—"

Niko spins around and covers Kota's mouth before I can do or say anything.

"*Shhhh!*" Niko hisses. He continues to press Kota's mouth shut as he looks around in all directions, as if he is waiting for something to happen.

After a few seconds, he lets go of Kota and again places his finger to his own mouth, this time looking at both of us, before turning back toward the building.

In the faint glow of the moonlight, I can just see the door, but there are no windows the closer we get, which makes the building look like a bunker designed to keep something locked away. By the time we reach the door, the mystery of what this place might be only deepens because there isn't a single clue that alludes to what it might be.

Niko pulls a chain from beneath his sweatshirt, revealing a heavy key dangling from it. He slides it into the lock with precision, but for a moment, he pauses to press his ear to the door, as if listening for something beyond it.

None of us moves, and the silence stretches before he abruptly turns the key and swings the door open.

"*Inside,*" he whispers, his voice low and urgent. Then he waves us through without another word.

A sharp click slices through the silence as the door shuts, and the small entrance is suddenly bathed in light. The space is surprisingly cramped, no larger than Irene's place, despite the large exterior of the structure we just saw. A desk sits in the corner, cluttered with a similar radio to the one in Irene's place. Beside it is a towering stack of neatly piled, laminated papers, the edges slightly curled as if they've been handled countless times. To the left of the desk is a second door that seems to lead deeper into the structure, but my instinct tells me that's a threshold we're not going to cross.

"Aurora . . ." Niko starts, his eyes full of shock and anguish. "I am so relieved you are alive! Jada and I were so worried."

He reaches out his hand to place it on my shoulder, but I pull away.

"Okay, I know you must have questions. I would too," Niko says. "But listen carefully. We only have a few minutes before I have to take you to the Hold Building, and I—"

"No," I say firmly. "I deserve answers. What is going on? How did you get here?! Why did—"

"Quiet!" Niko shouts back, before covering his own mouth in regret. "I don't have time to explain. We need to get to—"

"Why did you and Jada disappear? What happened?!"

"Aurora, I promise, it's not what you think," Niko says calmly, attempting to regain control of the moment. "We didn't want to leave you all alone. Jada and I had to leave because—"

Rage ignites inside me, spreading like wildfire until it claws at my throat. Without thinking, I shove Niko hard in the chest, sending him crashing into the desk behind him. His black walkie-talkie falls off his hip and to the ground, hitting the floor with a loud *THUD.*

"But you *left* me, Niko!" I scream, my voice breaking as the words fly out.

"Whoa. This is Niko?!" Kota blurts out in shock.

"Quiet!" Niko snaps, trying to regain his footing. But I don't let him.

"You left me all alone in that hellhole to die!" I scream, the tears finally breaking free. "What kind of person does that?!"

I go to push him again, but this time, he's ready. With a steady force, he grabs my arms and twists me around, pressing his chest to my back while his hands lock around my mouth.

"Aurora, we'll *all* die if you don't shut up," Niko grinds out.

As I struggle to break free, his grip tightens. "Just stop for a second and let me explain."

But I don't want to listen.

I want to make him feel the pain of what he did to me more than anything else. I want to—

"Aurora!" Kota says. "Give the man a chance."

I look over at Kota, who is cowering on the floor. Even in my rage, I can feel the tremor in his voice and the fear beneath his words, and it sinks me in an instant. I collapse, almost sliding through Niko's grasp, but he lowers me gently to the floor instead as Kota crawls over and hugs me.

"Aurora, you must listen to me," Niko begs, trying to catch his breath. "We didn't plan for any of this to happen."

"Like I am going to believe anything you say," I bark back while Kota leans deeper into me. "Why should I trust you?!"

"We don't have time to discuss this right now," Niko says, turning toward the door. "But the truth is we left you to keep you safe. It was the only choice!"

"You thought you would keep me *safe* by leaving me in a flooded house?!" I counter. "I had nothing! I was attacked, and I—"

A static, muffled voice rings out and fills the small room, shocking us all. Niko spins around, searching the floor until he finds his walkie-talkie and holds the top button.

"Shift One here," Niko says into the walkie-talkie, steadying his voice as he presses the button again.

"Shift One, are you almost to the Hold Building with the two kids?" a deep voice calls.

Niko looks down at the two of us, his eyes deep with concern.

"Yeah, just got a little turned around," he affirms. "On our way. Shift One, out."

Niko closes his eyes and puts the walkie-talkie on his hip as he takes a few deep breaths.

"Aurora," he says while closing his eyes for a moment, "I need you to trust me, and I need you to do exactly as I say. Can you do that?"

"Give me one good reason," I snarl. "One good reason to trust you."

Niko opens his eyes, and they move back and

forth, searching for something that might convince me to listen.

"Did you make it to the INCH Room?" he asks.

The question catches me off guard.

"Um, yes, I did, but only because—"

"Did you see your Bug-Out-Backpack there?" Niko continues speedily as he grabs the door handle. "The dark-green one, with all the extra supplies?"

I reluctantly nod yes.

"That was for *you,* Aurora," he says, squatting and putting his hands on my shoulders. "It was the last thing we could do to give you a chance!"

A chance. Just like Markell said. A chance.

Niko's eyes lock onto mine, making me feel the worth of every single word. It was the same thing I'd felt when Jada sat next to me on the mattress—something quiet and earnest, pulling us closer in a way that was hard to ignore.

There is a sudden shift, a new energy humming in the space between Niko and me, and I can't ignore it. In fact, I want to stay in it, whatever it is.

"Aurora?" Kota prompts. "Aurora, what are we going to do?"

I stand up and help Kota to his feet.

"Whatever he says," I respond. "We're going to trust Niko."

Niko breathes a sigh of relief at my agreement, then immediately shuts the lights off to the entrance and cracks the door back open.

"I don't want to, but I have to take you to the Hold Building for now," he says, his voice growing more tense. "I'll try my best to keep you together, but I can't promise anything."

"What's the Hold Building?" I ask as Niko sticks his head out the door.

Niko's grip tightens on the frame, like he is straining against something we cannot see.

"It's a prison," he mutters. "A horrible, horrible prison."

Chapter 32

A lump forms in my throat as we follow Niko out the door and back into the quiet night.

I want to regret putting my trust in him, but there is an earnestness in his voice. I've never heard him like this, ever. Not even on my makeshift birthday.

"One more thing before we get there," Niko whispers as we quickly move away from the building and down the dimly lit path. "Jada will be there, but you need to act like you don't know her."

"*Jada* is in there?" I whisper back firmly. "Why is Jada in the—"

Niko stops so quickly that I bump into his back, which makes all three of us stumble.

"Sorry about this," he warns. "But I have to. Just play along."

Niko ducks around behind Kota and me and grabs us each by the collar of our jackets.

"Get moving!" he yells angrily, suddenly becoming another person. "Move faster or I'll make sure you won't be able to walk at all!"

The change in temperament is impressive. Niko loosens his pull on my jacket, but not by much, and uses it to guide me down the trail as he continues to yell every few steps.

"I said, *shut up!*" Niko yells again to no one. "You should have said something to Irene when you had the chance!"

As we make our way back through the small, repetitive structures, I can't help but feel like we are being watched. Niko must think the same thing because his fake demands and anger become more frequent.

"Get moving, will ya?!" he bellows. "My shift ends in a few minutes, and I want to get some rest!"

A few windows illuminate as people click their lights on, probably wondering why there's a commotion in the middle of the night. Still, Niko continues his act, so while trying not to be too overly dramatic, I play along too.

"I'm not telling you anything!" I pull back on my hood. "Let me go!"

"I said, *move it!*" Niko hollers again, pushing my neck down before yanking me back up.

I catch a glimpse of Kota, who is either confused or terrified. Either way, his shocked face is selling it to the eyes in the windows as we pass by.

Niko continues to push us down the trail until the lights of the small village fade and we round the corner of a large rock, at least two stories tall. Braced against the other side of it is a large, skinny building, almost identical to the one Niko, Kota, and I were just in. However, this one has deteriorated and is on the brink of collapse. The roof is caved in slightly, and chunks of the siding are lying on the ground as if they have recently fallen.

Niko pushes us forward and knocks on the door.

"I'm working on a plan," Niko whispers quickly in my ear. "Just be agreeable to the guards, and stay quiet."

The door whips open after Niko finishes his final word, and two people, a man and a woman, take up the entrance.

"Just getting back from Irene's place," Niko says, shoving Kota and me forward. "Took us a bit because of their inability to follow directions."

The woman grabs Kota by the arm and pulls him inside.

"Sounds like this one should spend some time in the dark room," she says in a gleeful tone. "What do you think?"

"As much as I hate to say it, I would keep them together in a single cell," Niko says, pushing me forward. "The smaller one cries when he is away from this one. Unless you want to listen to wailing your entire shift, it's better to—"

"I get it," the man says as he grabs my hood. "I don't feel like having a headache when my shift ends."

I turn my head to try to catch Niko's eyes one

more time before he leaves, but he has already started back up the path, hopefully to work on his plan.

"Let's go, you two," the woman says as she begins to walk. "This way."

The man and woman lead us past the entryway into a hall lined with barred rooms, where the smells of damp concrete and mold fill the air. The hallway's end isn't visible due to the barely glowing bulbs hanging from exposed wires in the ceiling, which make the corridor seem like a never-ending nightmare. Broken pipes line the walls, dripping water into puddles on the floor, the sound bouncing off the cracked and stained surfaces.

We follow the couple as the man runs his hand against the rusted metal bars of each cell. I glance into one of them, and my heart sinks. A man sits slumped in the corner, his clothes hanging off him like they belong to someone twice his size. His cheeks are hollow, his skin pale, and his eyes . . . his eyes don't even look up as we pass. He's just staring at the floor.

Kota is a half step ahead of me, taking in the same sights, and I can tell by his pressed lips that he is fighting back tears. And the farther we go, the more people we see—some lying on thin mats, others huddled together for warmth. Although they appear stronger than the first man, they all have the same look on their faces: a broken one. Their spirits are frail, like a gentle breeze could snap them in half.

There's no yelling, no crying—no sounds of life at

all. Only the quiet shuffle of our feet echoing through the hollow space. I press my hands into my sides, trying to steady the unease rising in my chest as we move past more and more people.

We finally stop underneath the last of the lights before the hallway continues into darkness, and the woman removes a ring of keys from her large coat pocket. She flips through them idly until she finds one seemingly no different than the rest and opens the gated door while gesturing for us to go inside.

There isn't anything in the cell. No bed. No bench. No mat. It's just a cold, damp concrete cell.

"Get in," the woman demands.

Kota steps into the cell first, then me. The woman quickly shuts the cell door behind us.

"Never seen a kid here before," the woman says as she puts the keys back in her pocket. "You must've done something bad to end up here."

She shakes her head and turns to face the man, and then they both walk back toward the entrance. The clanging metal door echoes down the hallway, causing me to shudder as I take in everything around me.

"Aurora?" Kota says softly, his voice barely carrying over the sound of dripping water. "What are we going to do now?"

I don't have an answer. My mind keeps circling back to the same problem—there's no way out. The only hope I have right now is Niko.

But that doesn't stop the anxiety and fear from pushing in. I sit down next to Kota, who leans into my side as I press my forehead against my knees.

For a moment, it's just the sound of Kota's breaths.

Then, a movement. A rustling from the shadows of the cell next to us.

My spine stiffens.

Kota hears it too. He shifts closer to me, and I hold my breath as a face comes into the light between the bars of the connected cell.

"Aurora?"

The figure leans farther forward into the dim light. Her face is thinner than I remember, her eyes slightly sunken but still holding the same quiet strength.

"Jada?" My voice cracks.

My hands fumble forward, reaching—just to be sure, to believe she's real.

Jada catches them. Her grip is weak but steady, and a choked laugh slips from her lips.

"It's really you," she whispers.

Kota exhales sharply beside me. "You know her?"

Jada weeps. Kota scooches closer to the cell wall.

"I'm so, so sorry," she says as her tears hit the wet floor. "We were supposed to stay together. I didn't . . . I didn't know it was going to be like this."

I look out to make sure there are no guards, or anyone else who might overhear our conversation, but Jada doesn't stop.

"Aurora," she says, "I'm so sorry. Did you get the things we left behind for you?"

The words hit like a fist to my chest, just as they did when I saw Niko.

I pull back.

"Exactly," I say, barely more than a whisper. "You *left* me there. In that house. Alone."

Jada flinches, her eyes filling with something raw—guilt, regret, maybe both. She shakes her head.

"We didn't want to. We didn't have a choice."

"You always have a choice," I snap. "You made the choice to leave."

"We fought to stay with you," she says. "You have to believe me. We begged them! But they . . ." Her voice breaks. She swallows hard, forcing the words out. "They wouldn't allow it."

Something sharp lodges itself in my throat, but I push through it.

"Who is *they?*" I ask.

Jada is still holding my hand. Her fingers clutch mine like she's afraid I'll slip away.

"Okay . . . okay," she sniffles, wiping her face with her other hand. "You're right to ask questions. You need to know."

She looks over at Kota, who hasn't said a word yet, then continues.

"When Niko and I got into prepping years ago, we learned a lot in a short amount of time, mostly because of the radio contacts Niko made at the start.

They were so kind, so helpful, especially the more we got to know them. People not only from here but from all over the state. We just didn't know . . . we didn't know there was more to the group."

I squeeze my eyes shut, and my anger wrestles with something else—something more dangerous. The part of me that wants to believe her, like it wanted to believe Niko.

"Over the years, the prepping changed into something more: a plan for a safe place in the event that something horrible happened. And so Niko and I joined those plans."

"You helped create The Hill?"

"Yes, we did," Jada says, looking around the prison. "We gave our money, our time, our expertise. I helped design some of the earliest structures here, and Niko assisted with the infrastructure. Now I regret every part of it. When the rain started, the chatter in the group quickly shifted to when we would leave for The Hill. But not just that. We learned there were more people behind the scenes of The Hill. People who thought very differently about what it, and the others like it, should stand for."

"People like Irene?" I ask.

Jada nods.

"Niko and I hoped it would be different from what we'd heard," Jada continues. "But when we informed them we were bringing a third person—you—we were told no."

"No? Why?" I ask.

"Because you were not part of the planning," Jada informs me. "They said that only those who helped plan The Hill could come. And when they came"—Jada lets go of my hand to muffle her sobs—"in the middle of the night to get us, Niko was confident we could bribe them to get you a spot. We offered them everything we could think of, but they didn't accept. So Niko and I refused to go with them. We chose to stay."

I'm silent. Shocked.

"But that wasn't part of their plan. They said they needed our knowledge to continue with The Hill's operations. So they gave us *one* choice," she clarifies. *"Stand with The Hill, or do not stand at all."*

"I don't understand," I say, trying to catch her eye. "What does that mean?"

Jada takes a few short, sharp breaths in an attempt to control herself.

"They said if we didn't go with them quietly, easily, then they would kill you."

There is a lull for a moment while I try to make sense of what she says.

Jada takes another deep breath and continues.

"We had to leave you to keep you safe. It was the only way."

I scoot backward.

"It haunted me every single moment, not knowing if you were okay. Not knowing if we could have done something different," she says through more tears. "It happened so fast. They showed up in the middle of the night, and when we realized what was at stake, we had to move quickly. We left as many materials for you as we could in the INCH Room, hoping you would find them."

Her breath shakes as I sit frozen, watching her relive it all.

And I relive a moment too.

The men. The ones who broke into the mansion. Who threatened me. Who chased me.

They must have known I was there.

"Leaving didn't keep me safe," I mutter. "Two men broke in and tried to hurt me after you left."

Jada physically shudders.

"You have no idea what it was like for me," I say, my voice cracking. "I thought you didn't care. I thought you—" My throat closes up. "I thought you left me on purpose."

Jada sucks in a sharp breath, like I've struck her. She presses a hand to her mouth, shaking her head violently.

"No," she whispers. "Never! Aurora, you were the only thing we cared about. The only thing that mattered. We're not great at showing it . . . I never have been. But I promise you, we made all the decisions we could to keep you safe."

The room grows silent again except for the drip of water and the unsteady rhythm of my own breathing.

Kota shifts beside me, quiet but watching. Waiting to see what I will say next.

Jada hesitates, then reaches out again—tentatively, as if I might disappear.

"I know we don't deserve your forgiveness," she says softly. "I won't ask for it. I'm just so happy to see you're alive."

I stare at her, my heart hammering.

I want to hate her.

I *should* hate her.

She and Niko left me. They walked away while the water kept rising, while I was drowning in fear, while everything I knew got washed away. They were supposed to be my family. They were supposed to *stay.* They were supposed to protect me, right?

"We had to leave you to keep you safe. It was the only way."

I want to believe she abandoned me, because it makes the anger easier. But if she left because she thought it would save my life . . . then what should I do with all this pain?

Where do I put it?

I squeeze my eyes shut, pressing my nails into my shins. I can't stop the feelings from becoming something I don't want. Because if she's telling the truth, then hating her isn't as easy as I need it to be. If she's telling the truth, then she *did* fight for me. She *did* want me. And if I accept that, then I have to accept something even worse—

That maybe I would have made the same choice.

And I *did* make one like it. When I left Kota in the tree.

I glance at her, at the way she's watching me, holding her breath, waiting for me.

I look at Kota and think of the moments I wanted to protect him but couldn't.

All of it collides within me.

"I believe you," I say, trying my best to hold back my tears. "I believe you."

Before either of us can speak another word, the sound of clanging metal erupts through the hallway. Jada pushes away from the steel bars and retreats to the corner of her cell just as the two guards come into the light. I expect they are here to see me again, but I am wrong.

Instead, the woman takes the keys out of her pocket and opens the cell adjacent to ours, where a man is lying face down on the cell floor.

"To your feet!" the guard barks, but the man on the floor doesn't move.

"I said, *get up!*" the guard roars.

The man shifts his legs and then freezes in place.

"Not another one," the woman scoffs, putting the keys back in her pocket. "Let's take him to Irene."

The two guards stride into the cell and seize the man by his arms, hauling him upright. His head lolls forward as if he's barely aware of what's happening. With a rough yank, they drag him toward the hallway. His feet scrape and bounce against the floor, creating a sound I can only describe as heartbreaking.

The moment the heavy entrance door slams shut behind them, Jada presses herself against the barred wall and reaches out for me again.

I meet her hand with mine, gripping it tightly as if that alone could heal the anger and worry from all the moments I spent wondering if they ever really cared. With my other hand, I pull Kota closer until the three of us are pressed together, forming a small knot in between the cold cells.

None of us speak.

We just sit there holding on to one another, listening to the distant drip of water and the muffled sounds of the prison.

Chapter 33

The rest of the night, I drift in and out of sleep as I lean against the bars, holding on to both Kota and Jada. At times, I wake up almost in a fever dream: The room spins, the sounds bounce around in my head without any sort of cadence or order, and I struggle to see anything more than a few feet away from me.

But in those quiet moments, I feel a soft squeeze from Jada's hand. It's not strong, but it's just enough to pull me back. I look up and find her face, calm and steady, watching over me, making sure I'm okay until I drift off again.

It's not until morning that I feel fully present and confident that I'm not dreaming. Kota is sleeping but still pressed against me, his head buried into my side, and Jada is leaning firmly against the cell bars like they might allow her to break through.

"The guards will be here again soon," whispers Jada as I massage my face with one hand. "I'm sure Irene will want to speak to you again today."

I continue rubbing my face as I speak. "Okay,"

I mutter. "What about you, though? Why are you in here?"

Jada snakes her arm through a different section of the bars and puts it over my shoulder, and the comfort of it almost sends me instantly back to sleep.

"When we arrived, it became abundantly clear that The Hill was part of something we did not intend to create. That it was a dystopian movement. A societal shift."

"What exactly do they want to do?" I ask.

"We don't know all the details," Jada admits. "It was on the second day Niko and I were here, when I tried to help some drifters who were approaching The Hill." She motions to three women huddled against the far wall in a cell farther down the hall. "Even with my knowledge, which everyone said they needed to make this place function, I was jailed immediately for allowing others to join us. I didn't stand with The Hill."

"I don't understand," I say, still looking at the women leaning against each other, asleep. "Why is that acting against The Hill?"

"It's not an oasis," Jada informs me. "It was not made for just anyone to come. It is for an exclusive group, one that we didn't know we were a part of until it was too late. They have their own agenda. We think it's to create a—"

Jada is interrupted by the sound of the entry door, followed shortly by footsteps.

"Prepare yourself," Jada warns. "If they get you, just do as they say."

We separate. I turn to see the two guards pausing at a cell down the hall.

"I saw Niko yesterday," I say to her, trying to run my words together as fast as I can. "He said you would be in here. Said he was working on a plan. Are you revolt—"

Jada quickly hovers her hand over my mouth.

"I know about the plan," Jada whispers, "but you cannot talk about it here. We have to wait until—"

"Hey, you two!" a female voice booms from down the hallway. "What are you doing?!"

Jada shifts away from the wall, moving back toward the center of her cell as a man and woman walk down the hallway. When they step fully into the light in front of us, I notice the guards have changed. The woman is the same, but the man . . .

Niko!

"Get up, kid," Niko says with impatience, gesturing for me to move. "Time to see Irene. Hopefully you've got something better to say this time."

I push myself upright just as Kota stirs. His bleary eyes dart around the dim cell, trying to make sense of what's happening.

"I have to go," I murmur, steadying him against the cold iron bars.

"Wait . . . what?" Kota blinks rapidly, shaking off sleep as he scrambles to his feet. "I'll come too."

Niko's hand clamps around Kota's arm before he can take a step. "Oh, you're coming out of the cell too," he says in a flat tone. "But you're going in here."

The woman beside Niko steps forward and fumbles through her key set until she places one in Jada's lock. Her cell swings open, and before Kota can resist, Niko shoves him inside. Kota stumbles forward, colliding with Jada. For a moment, she locks eyes with Niko, as if they are having a conversation only they can understand, before she turns her attention to Kota.

"Aurora!" Kota's voice cracks as I step away, joining Niko and the other guard. "Don't leave me here!"

"I'm here," Jada says softly, placing a steady hand on his shoulder. "Try to save your energy, please." Her words are calm, but I can hear the exhaustion in them. I don't know if she's saying it for Kota or for herself.

Before I can say anything more, Niko pulls me away, and we march down the cold passageway back to the entrance.

"I can take it from here," Niko says to the other guard. "Make sure everyone stays in line."

There is a pause from the woman as she soaks in the command, but she shrugs and sits down at a desk, where a small computer lies next to a log of many numbers and names. I try to read the list, but Niko pushes us on through the door and into the morning light.

It takes a few moments for my eyes to adjust as Niko leads us around the building and past the massive boulder. When I finally blink away the haze, I'm greeted with a view of The Hill in full daylight, and the difference is staggering.

The eerie glow that made everything feel ghostly in the night is gone. Now, in the light, details emerge that I hadn't noticed before: the neat, covered flower beds hugging each hut; rows and rows of glass greenhouses built along the edges of the gravel path, packed with thriving vegetables; and clusters of brightly painted stones scattered across the grass like hidden gems, as far as I can see.

I wasn't expecting this, and I can't deny it. The Hill is beautiful.

Niko tugs on my jacket and guides me up the path as more of The Hill comes into view.

Adults are everywhere. Some are crouched in garden beds, carefully pulling weeds, while others stand outside their huts, chatting in low voices. A burst of laughter rings out from somewhere up ahead, mixing with the steady crunch of gravel under my feet as we climb toward Irene's place.

Then the stares begin.

Some people glance at me quickly before looking away, but others don't. Their smiles disappear, replaced with frowns or narrowed eyes, like they're not sure if I belong here. A prickly feeling crawls up my back, making me want to shrink into myself.

But as uneasy as their looks make me, something else is even worse. And even though I was told already, being confronted by it feels different.

There are so many adults—dozens of them—but not a single kid. Not one.

"Irene is going to try to get more information," Niko whispers in my ear. "She wants to know as much about you as possible."

"I don't have anything to share," I say, almost inaudibly. "She thinks I'm with a group."

We walk for a few more seconds before Niko adds something else.

"Just make sure to protect yourself," he says as we approach Irene's dwelling. "I need a few more days before we can execute the plan to—"

Irene's face, plastered with a sinister smile, appears in the barred window. In response, Niko gives me a hard shove in the back, forcing me to catch myself on the front door.

I gather myself just as the door opens to Irene, who is holding a plate filled with apple and orange slices. They seem to be glowing from the morning sun, something I haven't seen in months.

"Can you believe the sun is peeking out from the clouds today?" Irene says, almost giddy. "What a miracle of a day. Truly."

I don't say anything.

"You must be tired," she says, pointing inside. "Come. Sit down."

Niko begins to walk in with us, but Irene holds up a hand.

"You can stay out here and wait," she commands, her voice lowering. "This is a private conversation."

Niko nods and steps back with his hands folded in front of him. As Irene turns to shut the door, Niko catches my eye and offers me a small, delicate smile.

Why does she trust Niko if Jada is in prison? Doesn't she know they are together?

"Okay, let's have a seat," Irene begins. She guides me over to the table with the maps.

"We got off on the wrong foot yesterday," she says, pointing to one of the maps. "I can be a bit cold when The Hill needs protecting, and that's all I want to do: protect The Hill so we can protect the other ones."

"The other ones?" I ask before I can stop myself. "What other ones?"

"I know, it's hard to imagine." Irene points at the map. "How can a place like this exist without anyone knowing?"

I shrug.

"Careful, precise planning and prepping," she says boastfully. "That's how. All across the States, we have been waiting for the moment to put our plan into action. I honestly didn't think a disaster like this would happen in my lifetime, but now that it has, I am proud of what we have accomplished. Just look at this!"

Irene moves her hand across the map.

Hundreds of small orange dots cover its surface.

"See? Every single one of these is a part of The Hill. Places of refuge just waiting to be used in case of a worldwide apocalyptic event."

Her excitement grows as she moves over to a larger map.

"And here! See? More and more, all with the same values as us! Places to thrive and be happy while the rest of the world is in turmoil. Places to start over!"

My eyes scan the maps as I try to take in the total number of dots.

It's overwhelming.

"And to think I get to be a leader of one of these, connected to hundreds of others. What a blessing. A true blessing."

I lean over the map to get a better view.

"Are all The Hills like this one?" I ask, putting my finger on one of the dots. "Are they all the same?"

"Oh no, that wouldn't work very well." Irene laughs. "Different landscapes call for different plans. It's not like we predicted what would happen, you know. We just knew something would. We have a high place, so we built The Hill here, on my property."

"You *own* this land?"

"I do," she says boastfully. "And I am glad I could contribute to The Hill."

It's quiet for a second as I continue to scan the maps, looking for anything familiar, until a thought comes into my head I cannot silence.

"But what about all those people in the prison? What about people who need help?" I ask. "Why can't they be here?"

Irene takes the map beneath my fingertips, folds it, and places it back on the table. "You're inquisitive. That's a good quality to have."

There is a long pause as Irene clears off the rest of the table and places the plate of fruit in front of us.

"When you plan something as large as The Hill, you can only plan for the people that planned *with* you," she begins. "It's rule number one of prepping. *You prep for you, and no one else.*"

There it is again! That rule. But it doesn't make sense to me.

"If that is the number one rule, then why are there other people here?" I press. "Shouldn't you just be by yourself?"

"Another good question!" Irene remarks, nodding her head in approval. "I see your point, but if you find others that prep, plan, and believe in the same thing as you, why not team up and plan *together,* especially if you have time? And we've had plenty of time."

Irene leans back in her chair with an arrogant smile, like she just won an argument.

"But that doesn't mean you can't help people who come here," I counter.

Irene adjusts her position forward and presses her index finger onto the table.

"If I were to accept everyone who arrives," Irene says, "what would that do to this place?"

I don't answer.

"It would destroy it," Irene states, her voice becoming firmer. "Everything we have worked for. Everything we planned and prepared for. Everything we've built!"

Irene pushes the plate closer to me, but I don't move a muscle.

"Only a certain kind of person can handle the pressure of maintaining this place," she says, rotating one of the orange slices in the air before putting it in her mouth. "Take Niko, for example. He is loyal. He's given knowledge, time, and money, a lot of it, to make this place happen. He wants to *help* The Hill. His wife was like that too. Designing the dwellings, helping Niko with the grid . . . but she decided to help strangers who *didn't* plan with us, who *didn't* sacrifice their time and energy. It was *her* decision to go against The Hill, so a choice had to be made."

A choice . . .

"Niko could join her in the Hold Building with the rest of the rotting society," Irene taunts, "or he could continue in his loyalty to The Hill, the place he helped create. The place that *saved* him. And what do you think he chose?"

I know the answer she expects. The one she wants.

But I also know the truth.

Niko had to make a choice to protect Jada. If he was in there with her, they would have no chance to escape.

He is planning something. He has to be. He said so. Niko is always planning.

I have to believe Niko.

"I think he picked The Hill," I lie, as I pick up an apple slice off the plate. "Seems like an easy choice to me."

"Exactly! See, you understand," Irene smiles, pushing the plate toward me. "Look at everything we have been able to accomplish here, amid the chaos! Food, housing, stability . . . I am asking you to make the same kind of choice Niko made. Help me protect The Hill. Help us start something new, something *better*! Tell me about your group so I can protect us all."

I spin the plate as everything I have been through in the last month spins in my mind too: the mansion, Kota, the Dark Pools, the hatchet, finding food, the city, Markell.

"So, what will it be?" Irene presses. "Stand with The Hill, or do not stand at all?"

"I want to help," I lie as I continue to rotate the plate. "But I really don't have any information about any groups. It was just Kota and me, so we—"

Irene lunges across the table and slaps me in the face so hard I spill over the edge of my seat and onto the floor. Before I can make a move, Irene steps over me, grabbing me by the hair, and pulls me to my feet.

"I knew you weren't going to help!" She spits in my face as I struggle to keep my feet on the ground. "You are just like the rest of those drifters trying to find a place to stay. *They* weren't ready. But *we* were! You all just want to take The Hill for yourself! You're just another useless—"

The front door bursts open, revealing Niko, who is already sprinting toward us.

Irene lets go of my hair to defend herself, but it's too late. Niko delivers a punch to her face, the force sending her sprawling over the top of the table and onto the floor.

"Aurora, are you okay?!" Niko asks, shaking the pain from his hand as he helps me to my feet.

I look over at Irene, who is lying motionless on the ground.

"What did you do?!" I ask. "Is this part of the plan?"

"No," Niko says as he fumbles with the walkie-talkie on his hip. "But plans change."

He messes with the top dial until a low hum comes from the speaker, and he clicks the side button hard as he holds the walkie-talkie up to his mouth.

"Listen up, everyone. It's Niko," he begins, staring at me intently. "The revolt starts now."

Chapter 34

Niko grips my hand and pulls me against the wall near the entry door, his walkie-talkie pressed tight against his ear. I study his face, searching for any sign of panic, but there's none. He looks exactly like he did when the rain came, with a sharp focus that seems to compound with every passing second.

A crackle of static fills the silence before a voice comes through.

"Copy, Niko," the voice affirms. "Moving now. To the boats in three."

Niko exhales a short, steady breath, then turns to me.

"There are others here who don't agree with what The Hill is doing," he explains. "But there aren't enough of us to fight back. We have to leave, and we have to leave now!"

He spins toward the window, pressing a hand against the glass while clipping the walkie-talkie back onto his hip.

"Go where?" I ask, flicking my view back to Irene.

She's still on the ground but beginning to stir.

"The boats," Niko says, eyes locked on the outside. "They're the only way out."

A sudden chorus of shouts erupts in the distance, along with the sound of breaking glass. My pulse stutters.

"What about Kota and Jada?" I begin to panic. "How will we get them?!"

"It's okay," Niko says, his fingers fumbling at his side. "The guard from this morning should be letting everyone out right now. She's been helping ever since Jada was jailed."

He pulls back his jacket, revealing a hatchet strapped to his hip.

"Time to go!" Niko shouts. "Stay close!"

He yanks the door open, and we are instantly swallowed by chaos. The air explodes with the sharp thuds of bodies colliding. People are pouring out from their huts and spilling from the hidden doorways carved into the mountainside, their frantic movements blurring together, making it impossible to tell who is a friend and who might be a foe.

Then a loud wail cuts through the air.

Sirens.

I cover my ears and look up at the speakers mounted on the towering poles scattered across The Hill. Their piercing sound slices through the commotion, and for a split second, everyone hesitates—people freeze, eyes darting upward. Then, as if the sound itself reignites the panic, the fighting surges forward, even more frantic than before.

I am so caught up in the sight of it all, I don't realize that Niko is trying to pull me away from the hut.

"*Run!*" Niko commands. "This way!"

We veer off the gravel path, slipping into the narrow gap between two greenhouses. When we pop out the other side, the ground beneath us shifts from firm dirt to a field of dense, mossy grass, and each step becomes an effort to keep from twisting an ankle or toppling over. I try my best to press forward, staying close behind Niko as he powers through.

"Over there!" he shouts, pointing toward the water's edge, where The Hill slopes down and meets the dock. "That's our way out!"

A clear path stretches toward the shoreline ahead, but movement to my right yanks my attention away. A surge of people floods the area near the massive rock where the prison is located. Even from here, I can feel the desperation rolling off them, the urgency to fight or escape.

"They'll make it," Niko calls from ahead. "Stay focused!"

We barrel down the hill as the sirens continue to blare above the screaming crowds. As we get closer to the boats, I see there are already people on the docks untying the canoes and other boats from their posts.

"They're with us!" Niko yells. "Head for a canoe, any of them!"

It's a frenzy of splashing and yelling ahead of us as more people attempt to take a canoe. It's impossible to locate one that isn't occupied the closer we get, and soon the only thing that stands out is the motorboat Kota and I were brought in on by Aiken and his crew, which is tied to the dock with multiple thick ropes. It looks even worse in the daylight, but the closer we get, the more I think it might be our only option.

My legs lock in place as the choices and panic overwhelm me.

I don't want to go back out onto the water. I know what is out there.

I also know what is here.

Each seems just as bad as the other.

"Come on!" Niko yells, grabbing my wrist. "Aurora. *Move!*"

He leads me off the grass. As we hit the wood of the dock, a small group rounds the corner of a nearby building. My eyes lock onto one figure immediately, because the jacket is unmistakable.

"Kota, *run!*" I scream, my pulse hammering as the group moves closer to the water.

Jada's face comes into view as well. It's twisted with fear, next to others who wear the same expression—wide eyes, tense bodies, pure terror.

"Get in the boats!" Jada shouts. "They're coming!"

The words barely leave her mouth before a much larger crowd surges into view behind them. They move fast, too fast, and they're closing the gap with ease. The sunlight glints off their weapons of steel and edges: knives, axes, and brutal handcrafted tools.

"In the bigger boat, *now!*" Niko orders, his voice cutting through the panic. He turns sharply toward a woman crouched near a wooden crate. "Hand me one of those!"

Without hesitation, she reaches in and pulls out a small dark-green cylinder, no bigger than a can of pumpkin pie mix. Niko snatches it from her hand and bolts forward, his arm whipping back and launching the object high into the air. It sails over Jada, Kota, and the others, then vanishes into the group coming up behind them.

A heartbeat later, an explosion shatters the air. The ground quakes beneath us as a thick wall of smoke erupts, swallowing the view of the charging crowd in an instant. Screams and cries rise up with the smoke as Jada's group stumbles forward.

"That was the last one," the woman informs Niko as he runs back. "We need to leave!" She frantically turns and jumps in a canoe, and more and more people join her. There is clanging and shouting as each canoe attempts to weave its way out past the dock and the others, with no order or clear path ahead.

"Aurora!" Kota's voice cuts through the roar. Before I can react, he's already reaching for me. His arms wrap around my waist, and I pull him close, gripping the back of his jacket as hard as I can.

For a moment, everything around me fades—the shouting, the stomping feet, the sheer terror pressing in from all sides.

But then a deep, guttural chant swells over me, rolling down The Hill like an avalanche.

My heart clenches as I look over Kota's shoulder.

A third group is descending.

Larger.

Faster.

Their bodies are packed tightly together, moving like a rogue wave heading to shore.

And at the front, face knotted in fury, is Irene.

I look around to see what options we have. Not a single canoe is left. They are all either being fought over, or already occupied in the open water.

"Go! To the big one!" Niko shouts again, already springing into the large boat and gripping the wheel.

Kota, Jada, and I don't hesitate. We leap the gap between the dock and the boat, landing hard enough to send the vessel rocking.

Niko turns the key.

Nothing.

He twists it again. The engine sputters, coughing like a dying animal, but it refuses to roar to life.

"Come on!" Niko growls, jamming the key forward again.

Nothing.

It's too late. The mob has reached the dock.

A thunder of feet slams against the wood, rattling

the planks. They flood forward with their weapons raised, gleaming knives and rusted axes all ready for attack.

A man vaults onto the dock and hurls himself at the canoe next to our boat, one hand clawing at the edge while the other swings a blade down onto the person in it.

A woman barrels into another, pushing her out of the canoe and clipping her head with the end of her bat.

Then, a man reaches us.

He jumps swiftly over the gap to land in the boat, but Jada kicks out hard, her foot slamming into his chest. He lets out a choked grunt as he tumbles backward, crashing into the water between the boat and the dock.

To our left, part of the mob pushes into the water, tipping over the other escaping canoes and the people within them.

Another man swings a crowbar at our hull, and a sharp *CLANG* rings out. Kota stumbles backward and falls to his knees while Niko runs to confront the attacker. Meanwhile, I lunge forward, grabbing Kota's arm and yanking him up just as a woman seizes the side of the boat and begins to haul herself up.

Before she can fully get in, I grab an oar from the floor and slam the handle into her hands. She shrieks and releases her grip, falling backward onto the dock.

I turn to see Niko land a punch to the throat of the attacker with the crowbar as Jada takes the helm of the boat.

"Come on, come on!" she yells, twisting the key so hard I think it might snap.

The boat comes to life, and the force of the motor nearly knocks me off my feet. I scramble for the side, gripping the edge as we begin to speed away from the dock. The furious screams of the mobs grow in intensity behind us.

But just as relief floods my chest, the boat jerks violently, slamming to a halt so abruptly my knees buckle. The world spins, my shoulder crashes against the side of the boat, and Kota topples into me.

"What—?" I gasp, gripping the edge as the boat whips sideways, the momentum twisting it back toward the dock.

"We're still tied to the dock!" Niko shouts.

Before I can react, the boat slams against the large wooden beams of the dock with a bone-rattling thud, nearly throwing Kota and me overboard.

Immediately, more attackers rush at the sides of the boat, and one of them is ahead of the rest.

Irene.

"We need to cut it loose!" Niko roars, fumbling at his side for his hatchet.

Jada is already moving, reaching for the rope with shaking hands. But she's not fast enough.

A man from the mob swings a jagged piece of

metal at her, missing her by inches as she stumbles backward with a yelp. Kota lunges forward, shoving the man away, but another takes his place instantly as his hands grasp for Kota's jacket.

Irene grabs the rope and begins yanking us closer, closing the gap between the boat and the dock inch by inch.

No, no, no!

I glance around, looking for anything I can use to help.

That's when I see it, resting next to my backpack against the frame of the boat.

My hatchet!

Without thinking, I lunge for it, my fingers curling around the wooden handle so tightly it's as if it never left my grip.

I push myself to my feet as Niko fends off another attacker from the side and Jada does the same from the back, and I run to the front to cut the rope. Then I draw my hand back and bring it down in one swift motion.

But Irene's hand appears, shooting up from the side, and halts my swing.

I struggle against her, our hands slipping over the handle as I try to regain control. She's frantic as she yanks our arms back and forth, digging her fingers into my wrist hoping to free my hatchet.

I grit my teeth, refusing to let go.

Irene squeezes even harder and yanks my arm

to the side, ripping the entire sleeve of my jacket off my arm.

And then, something unexpected.

Irene stops, her gaze shifting to my forearm, and her hands loosen.

Her determined eyes meet mine. I use the opportunity to pull away, but instead of fighting, Irene steps back on the dock, her mouth open slightly, her face draining of color.

"It can't be," she says, her voice raw with disbelief. "I know . . . *I know* you!"

My heart skips a beat, and I glance down to my exposed arm. My birthmark—the three large dots I've always called Orion's Belt—is the only thing she could have seen.

"Cut the rope!" Niko orders as a man crashes into the water next to me. "*Now!*"

I snap back to the danger of the situation and bring the hatchet down with all the force I have left, slicing through the rope with incredible ease. The boat jerks free with a violent jolt, reversing away from the dock as Irene is left standing there, watching, her eyes still wide, still stunned.

I stand with my hatchet, staring back at her with the same expression.

Irene . . . knows me?

How?!

The boat slams against an adjacent canoe, breaking my gaze on Irene and directing it toward Kota, who is clinging to the seat next to Niko as he attempts to navigate through the hordes of people hoping to escape alongside us.

"Not the forest!" Jada yells above the motor to Niko. "Head north!"

Niko spins the wheel ninety degrees to the left, creating a small wave that pushes the other escapees to the side.

"Look out!" Kota declares, standing and pointing ahead. "Shui gui! Shui gui!"

As if things couldn't possibly get worse, the water all around starts growing dark-black circles that begin to merge together, rapidly growing in size.

"What is that?!" Niko yells.

I whip around, my breath catching in my throat.

The other vessels scattered around us begin to disappear as paddles thrash and desperate hands claw at the water's surface. Another canoe veers too close to a swirling void, and its front end dips suddenly into the abyss. Screams split the air as the boat is yanked downward, vanishing in an instant.

"They're everywhere!" Jada shouts, gripping the edge of our boat as the shifting black masses pulse outward, like ink seeping through paper.

More canoes tip as the passengers scramble across one another, some trying to leap to safety but finding nothing beneath them except darkness.

"Here. Grab this!" I scream, grabbing a paddle and plunging it into the water in the hopes that someone will be able to grab it, but none of them are close enough.

Niko grits his teeth as the boat curves and swirls around each growing Dark Pool.

"Hold on!" Niko shouts.

I manage to grip the rim of the boat and spin around. What I see steals my breath away.

Behind us, the water is a battlefield of chaos and despair. Canoes tip and vanish into the swirling voids, swallowed whole as if they had never existed. People thrash in the water, screaming, their hands reaching, before they, too, are dragged under. The Dark Pools spread like living shadows, devouring everything in their path except the few lucky canoes that outmaneuver them.

The engine roars, and we lurch forward again, skimming over the waves.

I can't look anymore. I don't want to see who won't make it, who I'm not able to save.

But before I turn away, something catches my eye.

Irene.

She stands at the edge of the dock, unmoving amid the chaos.

Bodies push past her, desperate hands claw at the dock for help, but she doesn't flinch. She doesn't help any of them. Her eyes are locked on us.

No.

On *me.*

I can tell they're on me. Even from a distance.

I hold her gaze until she becomes nothing more than a speck on the horizon, smaller than a pinprick on an empty page. Until the only things that remain are the water and the growing distance between us.

Epilogue

It's been four days since we left The Hill.

Niko, Jada, Kota, and I are still in the boat, or what is left of it. We've found unique ways to patch the emerging holes that keep letting in water, and the engine makes its own decision on when it will run and when it will suddenly stop.

But we are alive.

"How many cans do we have left?" Kota asks as he flicks some rubble off the edge of the boat and into the water. "Can I eat another can of pasta?"

"We can't eat whenever we want," Niko says from behind the steering wheel of the boat. "We need to conserve as much food as we can until we find something else."

"We are lucky to have anything," I remind Kota, pointing to the bag on the floor. "If Markell's bag hadn't still been in the boat, we would have nothing."

Kota moans and retreats under the cover of the torn tarp we've draped across the back of the boat. The canned food, and how much of it we eat, is the only thing we can control right now, as we fight a new ailment that beats down on us worse than the rain ever did.

The rain has stopped. And the sun has returned.

"Aurora, please try to stay in the shade," Jada advises. She is sitting under the shadow of the small awning just above Niko, tending to a wound on her arm she sustained during the riot. "It only takes a few minutes for your skin to completely burn."

She's right.

For the first time in months, the clouds have vanished, but the harsh sun is quickly changing the flooded world into something much different, and from what we've seen so far, much worse.

"Come join me," Niko suggests. "You can steer."

I squeeze next to him, and we share the sliver of protection the awning provides. He guides my hands to the correct position, and I wince as my fingers clasp the wheel. The tops of my fingers are already sunburned to bright red, and they ache when I clench them. My only relief is to occasionally step out into the sun and submerge my hands in the water, which doesn't seem worth it afterward.

"They look worse than before," Niko points out. "Let me help."

He retrieves a small empty can from the bottom of the boat and dunks it beneath the steaming surface of the water around us. He rejoins me at the helm and then slowly drips the water over my knuckles.

"Thank you," I say, slowly breathing out the pain. "That actually feels good, even though the water is warm."

Niko nods as he continues to move the steady drips across my hands, and then he brings up the question he's asked me every day since we escaped.

"So, you really don't know Irene?" he says, moving the stream of water to my other hand. "Can you think of *any* reason she might know you?"

It's the question I've had on my mind every waking second.

No one really knows me.

I've never really had anybody.

I have no idea who she is or why she stopped attacking me. She is as much a mystery to me as the earth's behavior is.

"Shoot," Niko says before I can respond. "I think there's another sign up ahead."

The announcement gets everyone's attention. Kota and Jada join Niko and me, and we try to make as much room for them in the shade as possible. Just ahead, sticking up from the water, is a half-standing structure, perhaps part of a billboard or large interstate sign.

"Can you make it out from here?" Jada asks, peering over from the protection of the shade. "Is it another one?"

"I think so," Niko says. "If it is, we'll head in a different direction."

It's quiet until Kota reads what we were all hoping wasn't there.

"Stand with The Hill, or do not stand at all," he mutters.

Then, out of nowhere, we hear it, bouncing across the water like it's been chasing us for days.

Sirens. Many of them.

Niko takes the wheel from my hands and jerks it hard to the left, toward the mountains peeking out just over the horizon.

"Get down!" Niko instructs, and we all rush to resume our positions in the shade. Out of sight, and out of the sun, as Niko presses the throttle to full speed.

We are running, but we aren't broken.

The four of us on this boat have more going for us than anyone on The Hill ever did.

We are together. We have each other.

And we care about one another.

And maybe, just maybe, that will be enough to make it.

But we will have to outrun *them*—and the sun—first.

About the Author

Matt Eicheldinger wasn't always a writer. He spent most of his childhood playing soccer, reading comics, and trying his best to stay out of trouble. Little did he know, those moments would ultimately help craft the first book in his debut novel series, *Matt Sprouts and the Curse of the Ten Broken Toes.* Matt lives in Minnesota with his wife and two children, and he tries to create new adventures with them whenever possible. When he's not writing, you can find him telling students stories in the classroom or trail running along the Minnesota River Bottoms.

You can learn more about him, his books, and his other adventures at *matteicheldinger.com* and on social media *@matteicheldinger.*

Acknowledgments

The idea for the *When the Rain Came* trilogy came to me while I was camping with my family. Without much warning, the sky turned dark, and we were suddenly caught in a heavy downpour, which forced us to stay inside our small pop-up camper for a good portion of the day.

It was there I wrote the plot for this entire series.

So as strange as it sounds, I need to thank the rain first. It has been an endless source of inspiration for me, aside from just this series. From running through downpours to experiencing the power of a single storm, the rain is what makes me feel the most connected to nature—and the most terrified of it.

There are also many people I'd like to thank for helping to make this YA debut trilogy a reality.

To the entire team at Andrews McMeel Publishing: You have provided a space for me to explore what type of author I want to be, and your confidence in my work has allowed me to do multiple projects I didn't think were possible initially.

Thank you for helping this teacher find his voice outside the classroom.

To my editor, Erinn: We have worked on many projects together, but working on this one with you has been my favorite.

To my agent, Dani: We have accomplished so much together in such a short time! I am proud to work with such a dedicated, supportive, and kind individual, and I look forward to whatever project we decide to tackle next.

To my wife, Briana: Your questions during our afternoon walks, when I typically regurgitate everything I am writing and thinking about, help refine my direction for both plot and character. You may never admit it, but I think you'd make a fantastic editor.

To my kids: Adventure comes in many forms, and I am so glad we get to do all of them together. You inspire me every day to write about what is most important: family.

To my readers: I am not sure I can adequately express my gratitude for your support of my work. Please know that I appreciate all of you, and I hope to meet you all someday. Thank you.

The rain took everything.
The sun will test what's left.

Aurora and Kota's journey continues in
When the Sun Returned.

Look for it wherever books are
available, starting Fall 2026!

Listen to *When the Rain Came*, available wherever audiobooks are sold!